NOTHING NICE TO SAY

A NOVEL

STEPHANIE WEBER

Weasel Press

Nothing Nice to Say
Stephanie Weber

ISBN-13: 978-1-948712-61-3

Weasel Press
Lansing, MI
https://www.weaselpress.com

Stephanie Weber is a comedian and writer who has been published in *Reductress, Bustle, The AV Club* and more. She performs at The Lincoln Lodge and Chicago Underground Comedy and works as a staff writer for Mr. Skin. Her play MARIA GARCIA IS HAVING YOUR BABY was nominated for the 2013 MetLife Nuestra Voces Latino Playwriting Award.

Twitter: @steph_eloise
Instagram: @steph_eloise

www.stephanieweberwrites.com

NOTHING NICE TO SAY

ONE

"Are you sure you want to do this?" Lisa asked Jose as they stood outside Cafe Mustache on a balmy September night. They peered inside the hip Logan Square cafe. It was dim, with various vintage signs and quirky art hanging from the dark, gray walls. Cabaret tables and a mix of coffee and cocktails to keep patrons buzzed in any way possible while they took in whatever performance was unfolding on the stage at night. Jose always thought it was reminiscent of the cool Greenwich Village folk clubs from the sixties.

Or so he thought. He wasn't alive then and those places were not the same as the books and movies like *Inside Llewyn Davis* would have him think. They were crawling with tourists now - not cool, turtlenecked bohemians. That was New York in the sixties. This was Chicago in 2013. It was a different place, but it was the place to be.

Jose looked into the big cafe windows to see a packed audience filling a low-key comedy show. The male comedian greeted the audience from the stage with lanky arms outstretched and a goofy grin that let the crowd know they were in on the joke. It was Arnie Palermo. Jose knew Arnie. Jose also knew the woman of the hour, the woman for whom this show was.

"I don't know if I want to do this," Jose answered his friend's previous question.

Lisa, his bandmate and best friend, nudged him. He shook his head, suddenly feeling nervous being so close to Sophie. He wasn't sure why. He had been close to her a million times, but now things were different. He had left her behind and had come back for her. She had no idea he was here.

"What? I don't know if I can do it, Lisa—"

"We came all this way!"

"I know. I know, but..."

He peered back into the venue. The crowd was laughing. The small stage in the back corner was the brightest spot in the dim, kitschy cafe. A "happy birthday" banner hung on the shimmering red "curtain" that was really just a shiny red sheet nailed to the back wall. It was an inviting little show and it was perfect for her, for his Sophie.

"...What if she doesn't love me anymore?"

Hearing himself say those words out loud made it a real possibility. He hadn't actually entertained that while he was on the road. He thought about her incessantly. He thought about what he had left behind and why. Yes, he wanted to make it as a musician - more than anything - and he absolutely knew the band was going to make it. But was it worth leaving her behind? Was it worth leaving his darling Sophie back home in Chicago? He didn't think it was.

"Jose. Do you love her?"

He nodded. "Yes. So much."

Lisa handed him the acoustic guitar. She smiled proudly. His friend seemed genuinely happy for his romantic pursuits. She encouraged him even when they were in a rusty van in Buffalo, New York. She encouraged him when they did shows in putrid Omaha basements. She encouraged him to leave their new, cramped band headquarters in Brooklyn and come back to Chicago to ask Sophie to come back to him. Hell, if he wasn't so in love with Sophie maybe he could have been in love with Lisa.

He grabbed the guitar like it was his weapon and he was about to go into battle. This was the weapon he needed to win back her affection.

"You're right, Lisa. I have to tell her how I feel. I have to tell her what I never told her."

"Man, this is so cool," Lisa said. "This is the stuff love stories are made of."

"It's now or never!"

With that as his battle cry, he strummed a chord on his guitar and heard the strings ring into the night air like the coo of a dove. Lisa opened the door to the cafe. The ruddy-faced doorman sat on a stool and asked for their ID's.

"It's five dollars and - hey, wait, where are you going? Where is he going?"

Jose didn't stop to bring out his ID or money or anything. He barely even looked at the burly guy on the barstool. With the guitar firmly placed in his hand, he glided right along as if these were moves he had choreographed. He had choreographed all of this a million times in his head while sitting in the tour van from New York City back to Chicago, visualizing everything he would say to her when he was face-to-beautiful-face. This is what he prepped for. This is what it all was for. He was going to get her back.

As he walked into the showroom he could hear her best friend and fellow comic Arnie introduce Sophie: "Please welcome to the stage the woman of the hour, the birthday girl herself: Sophie Martin!"

His angel stepped onstage, smiling at the crowd with her berry-colored lips. Her trademark berry lips. The lips that he once knew like a second language. The lips that tasted so sweet, that he missed so much.

"Hello, everyone! Keep it going for Arnie..."

She paused. She saw Jose walking into the room with his guitar. The applause from the excited, young crowd of hipsters and eager comedy nerds dissipated. The applause gave way to Jose strumming an acoustic ditty. A song that he had written for Sophie when they first met eight months ago.

"Jose?" she asked as she stood in front of the microphone stand. Her face had fallen. Her hazel eyes watched with a mix of caution and...what was that? Surprise? Horror? No, it couldn't be horror. Not for him!

"Sophie, I thought I wanted to leave town and go on the road like a real musician, but when I was out there on the lonely road - somewhere miles outside of Pittsburgh - the only thing that I could think of was you. I came all this way to celebrate you, on your birthday, and tell you I love you. I love you so much."

The crowd melted with collective "aws" like it was a heartwarming scene in a live taping of a sitcom. They were smiling, rosy-cheeked, as they individually turned their attention toward her to see what she would say. Would she have him? Would she accept his gesture?

"So, Sophie, what do you say? Want to give this thing another go?"

That mixed look on her face? It turned to straight up anger.

"What the fuck?"

Jose was taken by surprise. This was certainly not a part of his plan. That reaction was never the one she uttered in his daydreams when he went over all the different ways to win her back.

"You seriously interrupted my show—my *birthday* show—with some weird grand gesture like this?"

Jose couldn't believe what was happening and his shock felt a lot like anger. He was starting to get mad at her now.

How dare she be this ungrateful? He broke her heart - was she not pining over him? How could her feelings change like this?

"Yeah, what I'm doing is sweet. You know like that song 'Hey There Delilah'—"

"No, it sucks. It's selfish."

"Selfish—" he scoffed, but she zoomed over him, finishing her train of thought like he didn't exist.

"You left town three months ago. You never once called or texted me. And you think what? I'm going to be overjoyed to see you - on my fucking birthday?"

Yes, that was what he thought. Maybe the birthday was a bad touch. He thought it would be a kind of cool gift, but perhaps his little comedian wanted to have this day all to herself.

"Okay, I get that it's your birthday—"

"No, this is like throwing a surprise party for someone."

"It *is* a surprise, but surprise parties are kind of nice—"

"Shut up. Let me talk. This isn't for me. It's not about me. It's about you doing this weird attention-grabbing thing. You never talked to me. You never indicated you were thinking of me. Instead you storm into a show that people paid for to lay down your feelings like I'm in on the joke. I'm not in on the joke, Jose. This is barely about me. It's about you trying to feel like a good person in some weird rom com fantasy you concocted when your dick was dry in Pittsburgh—"

"*Outside* of Pittsburgh—"

"You never stopped to think how I would feel. Did you?"

He was silent. Her eyes were steadied on him like she was aiming a rifle. He felt like he might turn to stone.

"You can't just give someone radio silence and then come back like it's no big deal."

Lisa, having dealt with the doorman and paid for both of their tickets, stepped into the showroom. She shouted from the back, "Doesn't he get points for trying?"

A couple audience members grunted in agreement, but for the most part people either shook their heads or shut up. They didn't realize their five-dollar ticket to the comedy show would come with all this drama.

"Oh my god, points?!" Sophie said. She took the mic off the stand as if she was about to launch into an even harder tirade against Jose. "I didn't realize this was a game. Who are you? Who is that back there?" Sophie squinted toward the back to see, but Jose wanted to regain control of this situation.

"Look, I believe in love—"

"I told you I loved you and you cried."

An audience member "awwwwed" at that little anecdote. But no. It wasn't a beautiful moment. It was a strange reaction that ended in an argument, one that pissed off Sophie and made Jose realize that he had to be more vulnerable and in-touch with his feelings. Sophie just wanted a man who was already at that point and didn't need her to lead him there like a lost puppy on a leash.

"No, it wasn't cute," Sophie snapped at the person she couldn't see in the dark. "He cried and said 'Why would anyone love a tortured soul like me?' And then he never said it back. Then he just left. So, no, I'm not going to get back together with you just because you showed up and did something cute."

"But I'm a changed—"

"Spare me," she said. "You'll be back to your emotionally unavailable ways in three days. Tops."

Jose had no idea what to say at this point that would prove her wrong. He was asking her to blindly have faith in him. He hoped her love for him would make that leap of faith, but he didn't realize she torched her affection for him in the exhaust pipes of his tour band.

"Besides, I have a boyfriend. Something you would know if you spoke to me at all."

Sophie extended an arm to the corner just off-stage. A tall, burly man in thick-framed glasses was standing there. He waved sheepishly. Jose could practically smell the whiff of wannabe comedian off of him.

"Hey, what's up, dude? I'm Matt, the boyfriend."

This was the guy? Really? This guy was going to win over him? Jose stiffened up his posture and took on an almost unconscious macho stance like some kind of animal instinct that kicked in to protect what was once his.

"Not much, Matt. Just trying to win back my girl—"

"Okay, don't bond!" Sophie yelled, still talking into the mic. The mic made everything she said sound powerful, like a proclamation. He felt like a peasant in the audience, addressing his majesty with a bleeding heart that she was stepped on from her pedestal.

"You're seriously not going to take me back," he said. "Even with an audience here and everything."

"Okay, that's manipulative."

"That's bullshit!" It was an immature thing for him to say, like he was a teenager getting detention for something he didn't do, but he couldn't think of anything clever. She was the funny one, the one with a way around words, not him. If he couldn't win her back with music - his language - then maybe he should abort the mission.

"I don't want to get back together with you. End of story—"

But he couldn't let it end like this. He couldn't. No way, no how.

"You know what I think, Sophie? I think you only care about yourself. You only care about yourself and your stupid comedy career. I hope it goes nowhere. I hope you're lonely forever because that's the only thing you care about."

She stared back at him in silence. He got her. His words managed to pinch her in just the right way. He knew the button to push: the comedy career. She nodded at him, looking down from the stage. In that moment she reminded him of a queen. Her fingers gripped the mic with grace, like it was a scepter. Her berry lips were pressed together tightly. Her eyes pinned him in his spot. Finally, she spoke evenly, and without any of the comedic effect that she was prone to when in front of a crowd.

"Even if that's true. It doesn't change the fact that I get to decide whether or not I want to date you again, and I don't want to."

A few audience members snapped. Cool. So now she gets to be a feminist hero? This could not have gone worse. Jose retaliated by shouting, "You're a bitch!"

"Cause I don't want to date you?"

"Yeah."

And with that he turned around, excusing himself and the clunky guitar from the audience members that had packed in to get a good look at this show. Everyone was on his side at first, but now they had turned against him. People started booing him. Lisa followed him out. The door closed behind them with the doorman muttering something about how they can't be readmitted.

Jose breathed in the city air. Chicago was always crisper than New York. It had felt good to be back even for an hour, but now he wanted to get the hell out of dodge. The only place he wanted to be was Brooklyn, a place that had no Sophie Martin.

A group of be-spectacled teenagers bumped into them on their way out. Jose turned around and yelled, "That show sucks! Don't go in there!" after them.

Lisa patted him on the back. "It'll be okay, dude."

"What the fuck do I do now?"

"I don't know. We'll move on and forget about her. It's not like she's actually going to amount to anything anyway. She's a nobody."

TWO

Five years later

The alarm clock rang on her phone. Sophie's eyes sprang open. She had laid down for a nap at three and now it was seven. She had a date at seven. And a show at eight. Fuck.

Sophie swore to herself as she got up and looked in the mirror at the purple sweater dress and gray tights she had fallen asleep in. This would have to do. She stuck gold hoop earrings into her ears and put on her berry-colored lipstick. She smacked her lips together and pursed at herself in the mirror. That lip smack was one of her favorite sounds in the world.

She grabbed her leather purse that could no longer close, so things were always flying out of it. She flung open her bedroom door to see her roommate Sumi in the living room. Great. The person she was trying to avoid this week until she got enough money for rent.

Sumi, her gorgeous roommate with long raven hair, stared at her incredulously.

"You got that rent yet?"

"Huh? Oh, yeah."

Sophie grabbed her winter coat that was hanging on a

hook in the hallway and opened the door to leave.

"Wait! Are you leaving?"

"Yes, I have a date! And a show—"

"Sophie. Do you have rent? It was due three days ago—"

"Yes! I do! I'm so sorry, Sumi. I just really have to go now."

She ran out the door, leaving her roommate to swear curses at her behind her back. They didn't really understand each other. They were random Craigslist roommates who had been co-existing for the last year, ever since Sophie's breakup with her live-in boyfriend. It was a great, old, run-down place in an amazing location and her office manager roommate was frustrated by Sophie's more artistic lifestyle. Regardless, Sophie would have rent after tonight's show. In the meantime, she was scheming OKCupid for a free meal and had to meet her newest meal ticket tonight at a swanky Wicker Park restaurant.

She ran down Belden toward Milwaukee Avenue - the hub of the neighborhood. Their street ran directly across from Revolution Brewery, one of the coolest and most popular breweries in Chicago, and across from Cafe Mustache, which was her go-to for coffee and late-night independent shows like the one she had tonight. Arnie was standing outside Cafe Mustache having a cigarette when he spotted her.

"Sophie! Sophie Martin! What are you doing?"

"I don't have time!"

Arnie waved her over, but she really didn't have time. She had to jump on the blue line train to get to Wicker Park in a jiffy.

"I have a date!"

"But...we have a show."

"Put me up last!"

"Jesus christ, so *you* get to headline?"

"Love you!"

Sophie ran down the street to the train stop around the

corner. She ran past the Mexican restaurant and pancake diner to jump through the turnstile and onto the train. Luckily, she darted up the steps to the "world famous elevated train" (that was on the vintage posters for Chicago tourism and Sophie could never help herself in calling the el the "world famous elevated train") and made the next downtown bound train. She was only two stops away from her destination, but it was enough time for her to pull out her pocket notebook and write her setlist for tonight.

She started scrolling down the names of her jokes:

Tinder date.

Candy corn.

Hometown—

It suddenly felt like someone was watching her. She looked up from her notebook and saw a typical train creepster staring at her. His eyes were wide on her and his disgusting upper lip managed to curl into a smile without the bottom lip moving at all. His eyes fixed down to her chest, which was barely visible in her slight V-neck dress. She snarled in response. He smiled. Oh, yeah? Sophie wasn't one to be out-creeped and let some train masturbator ruin her night. He took her pen cap and bit down on it hard with eyes trained on him as if to say *this is what I'd do to your penis.*

He averted his gaze and got up to move to a different seat.

Just then the train operator announced, "Now approaching: Damen."

That was Sophie's cue to get off the train and run like hell across the street to her fancy dinner date at Cafe Robey, a very nice-looking cafe that she had looked through the windows at many times. Now she would sit there! That was the only thing she liked about online dating: she could trick men with real jobs - A.K.A. not comedians, musicians, actors or artists - to take her to real restaurants that yuppies who worked for tech companies got to go to. Ah, the luxuries of modern technology!

She ran as fast as she could down the stairs, wondering why the world-famous elevated train had to be this damned elevated. She fluttered through the turnstile and down the incredibly busy Damen Avenue until she arrived at Cafe Robey, where her kind-looking date had been seated for fifteen minutes waiting for her. Sophie checked her phone for the time. Fifteen minutes late? That wasn't bad for her.

Her redheaded date stood to greet her. He looked like a very sweet geek. He had very thick coke-bottle glasses that made his blue eyes look huge.

"Sophie?" he asked her when standing to greet her.

"I told you, I'd be late! I was half-expecting to come in and see you with another date."

"Fifteen minutes isn't enough time for me to pick up a strange woman. My game isn't that strong."

"I see. You needed twenty minutes."

They laughed at each other's jokes. Okay, not bad for first date banter. Sophie was impressed. Usually when she went out with "normies" they were pretty boring. So what was this guy all about?

For one, his name was Joey. An adult named Joey seemed like trouble, but he was actually really nice.

Dating for her was a struggle. For all comedians, really. It wasn't like Sophie couldn't get a date. She was confident enough and could talk to almost anyone, but dating as a female comedian was rough. The more "normie" boyfriends she had had - that is, guys who did not do or appreciate comedy, people with good and regular jobs, people with other interests - were attracted to the idea of a funny woman. But then they actually saw what she did. They were around the slog: the open mics, the shows in bar basements for six people, the bombing, the friends with troubling habits like drinking or doing cocaine. It became too much for men. Women were intrinsically trained in society to be supportive, so male comedians rarely had the same problem. They might complain that their cute little girlfriends weren't funny, but otherwise they were content. Their partners supported their funny guy as if they waved pennants at every punchline.

Men were different. Sophie had dated seemingly cool people like architects and philosophy professors who were so into the idea of her, but once they got to know her and what being a comedian actually was like...they got very turned off. They didn't like watching her bomb and debase herself. They didn't like having her test material on them or lift things from their conversations to use in her act. They absolutely hated becoming a joke. It didn't matter to them that the audience didn't know they existed. They knew. They knew and they grew to resent her. That was what usually happened with her.

She had dated comedians - many comedians - but that was rough. Currently her ex-boyfriend was doing jokes about her all over the country. Don't shit where you eat or you end up eating shit.

But this guy seemed...nice. And cool, despite the coke-bottle glasses that magnified his eyes to look like a muppet. The two hit it off splendidly talking about movies while Sophie kept checking the time to make sure she wasn't late for her show. She was so pleased with herself that she could get a good meal in before heading out the door and be entertaining all at once. It made her feel absolutely cosmopolitan.

But something crazy was happening. She actually liked talking to this guy. She went on at least on OKCupid dinner or lunch date a week and this one was fun. He liked a lot of the same movies as her and kept mentioning comedians he liked. And they were actually ones she liked. What was going on?

After he recited all of his favorite parts from the movie

Wet Hot American Summer, she leaned in and said, "You have really good taste in comedy. Kids in The Hall, Maria Bamford, Wet Hot. I'm impressed!"

Joey, her date with a child's name, shrugged. "I love comedy. That's why going on a date with a comedian is pretty exciting to me."

She grinned. She had heard that one before, but maybe this guy actually meant it.

"Usually guys are pretty put off by the idea of a woman being funnier than them—"

Joey feigned surprise like a southern belle who has just heard something shocking and sinful. He put his hand to his heart and said, "God forbid! A funny woman!"

She laughed. He was kind of silly. That was cool.

"Trust me. I've heard that before."

"It's so weird though, right? Like what's wrong with a funny woman?"

This was a subject she knew too well. Every female comedian knew it. "Well, we're taught - you know, in society or whatever - that men are supposed to be funny, right? It's, like, this caveman idea. Man make joke, woman laugh at joke. They bone. It sounds regressive, but it really feels like so many guys think it's unnatural for a woman to be funnier than them. It takes attention away from them. They are supposed to provide and they are supposed to provide laughs. If I'm providing the laughs then they feel...inadequate, I guess."

"Wow, you're a feminist hero! With every punchline you're punching the patriarchy."

She laughed again, even if it wasn't laugh-out-loud funny. "I don't think that's how my mother looks at it, but sure."

"I have to tell you: I love it. Actually, my older brother and his wife are both comedians, so I guess I kind of idolize that kind of relationship."

This was a surprise to hear. Certainly she must know

them. Why didn't he bring that up before? One would think that if you were on a date with someone who had the same profession as your family members, you would bring it up. At least that's what Sophie thought.

"Oh. They are?"

"Yeah, I've been around comedy for so long—"

"Here in Chicago?"

"No. In New York. They write for Colbert."

"For *The Late Show*?"

"Yeah, that's them!"

Joey smiled back at her like a dope. Her lips pursed together, barely hiding her jealousy at people she didn't even know. What the fuck was this. This normal guy had a connection *this big*? And he was just never going to say it? She took a sip of pinot noir and ran her lips across her teeth as if that cleaned the blood red stains on her teeth. She smacked her lips together as a kind of comfort before flashing her teeth in a flirtatious smile. She leaned across the table to show off a smidge of cleavage as she asked the dreaded question in show business:

"How did they get that?"

THREE

She ran like hell up Milwaukee Avenue to get to Cafe Mustache at 8:45. Forty-five minutes late wasn't so bad, right?

Fellow comic Simon was hosting the show wearing a shnazzy bow-tie like he always did as if he was working the Borscht Belt. He always overdressed, forcing everyone to acknowledge it as his schtick. Sophie found everything about him irritating, but she played along because he hosted nearly every show in town because of his game show host energy.

Her best friend and fellow comic, Arnie Palermo, was standing off-stage. Sophie nudged her way through the crowd - noticing that some people were noticing her, which made her feel proud. They should. She had been doing comedy in the city for seven years at that point. She was now a top player, a local headliner and semi-celebrity...at least to people who went to comedy shows, and even though she regularly saw those people she still wondered why they did it. *Why are you leaving your house and paying money to come see this thing I am trying to do for a living? What's wrong with you?!*

Simon was wrapping up a joke as Sophie spotted Arnie off to the side of the stage with his arms crossed, furiously watching Simon and hating his schticky performance as much as Sophie did. That's why they were friends: they hated all the same people. Arnie saw Sophie and smiled, but he kept his arms crossed. He still had to act like he was mad at her audacious move of coming *so* late to his show.

"You made it, little miss headliner," he said.

"Thanks for putting me up last."

"You were supposed to feature for me, but whatever."

"I'd bury you anyway."

He smiled. "Oh, yeah. Remind me why we're friends?"

"Are you all ready for your final comedian of the evening?" Simon asked the crowd. That was Sophie's cue to go up. She took off her coat and dumped it in the corner with other comedians' coats.

"I can't hear you! I said are you ready for your last comedian of the evening?"

The crowd cheered.

"Your next comedian is so great - she's a woman."

God, really? Sophie leaned over to Arnie, "And that's all, folks!"

Her insides twisted when she heard that. Great. She's a woman? That's what you want the audience to know about her? You want to warn them like they have to take cover and put away shiny objects so she doesn't get distracted?

Arnie whispered back in a cartoonish yokel voice, "Gee, ma, a genu-wine woman?! Outside in the nighttime?"

But Simon was on a roll. "She's so funny, super cute—"

"Keep it in your pants," Arnie said out loud, but only loud enough for Sophie to hear.

"He just said I'm cute. Cool, I can go home. That's all the validation I wanted!"

"Please put your hands together for Sophie Martin!"

Her name was the magic word that told her to put aside her snarky comments and get on stage. It felt like entering a bull pit sometimes. She was going into the lion's den and attempting to tame them all.

After the set she and Arnie sat by the bar. Sophie never really liked talking to people after the show. She felt that oftentimes only the weirdest people came up to her. Guys trying to hit on her, women oversharing stories from their own lives that they thought of during her set, people thinking Sophie wanted to be their best friend. However, she did her best to muscle through it. She knew she had to. She appreciated them coming - she was just not that into small talk with strangers.

Luckily, Arnie was the same way. Typically, the two of them hung out together after shows, holing up in the corner away from the crowds.

A girl leaving the theater touched Sophie's arm on the way out. She turned over her shoulder to see plump smiling girl who was just excited to see her.

"Great job! I loved the show."

"Oh, thank you so much." That was her standard response. She always said it with surprise like she never expected anyone to compliment her after a set - even when she knew she did well.

"Have a good night! I'm going to follow you on Twitter."

Sophie grinned as the girl left.

"What about my Twitter? I wasn't funny enough for the Twitter follow?"

"You were very funny, Arnie. That was probably just some solid girl power." Sophie lifted a peace sign and said "Girl power!" like a Spice Girl.

Arnie shook his head. "God, all of your references are from the 90's. How old are you again?"

"Twelve!" She waved at more people leaving and thanked them for coming.

"Okay, honey," Arnie said with a voice that indicated he was going to level with her. It was time for some real talk.

"Tell me more about this date!"

"Girl, bye."

"The dork has connections though!" he said.

"Isn't that a crazy bomb to drop?!"

"That wasn't a date. *That* was networking."

She had looked it up and it was real. It wasn't a line. His brother really wrote for the show.

"He was so nice," she said as if she was asked.

"But was he funny?"

Sophie pressed her lips together. "Welp."

"So no," Arnie said, answering his own question.

"He did quote a lot of funny things."

"No! He's a quoter?

Sophie nodded sadly. "I know, I know. Just quoting something doesn't make you funny. It just means you can remember things."

"I think that's a sign of autism," Arnie joked, taking a swig of his whiskey and coke. "Do you think you'll see him again?"

"Ugh, I don't know. I feel like I have to. Right? I have to somehow slip him my CV to give to his brother—"

"No! You can't date him if he isn't funny. You hate that."

"But you do it all the time."

"Yeah, because I love dumb, beautiful idiots," Arnie said. "You actually like funny guys. That's literally your only requirement whereas I like anyone who looks like Idris Elba with the brain of an ant."

"You're right," Sophie whined. "But I want to be on TV."

"Then suck it up! Is being funny really that important?"

They looked at each other with uneasy grins. They knew the answer, but it was so hard to find that perfect, beautiful, funny person who wasn't boring as shit or worse - threatened by them.

"If they aren't funny, they're boring."

"Only boring people are boring," Arnie said.

"Is that a lyric in 'Flagpole Sitta?'"

Arnie stared at his best friend like she had grown a second head and the second head was less attractive. "Okay, what year is it and why is your brain retaining all the lyrics to some shitty song from 1998?"

"97."

He rolled his eyes. "I'm starting to see why you're having trouble dating."

She shook her head. "I don't think *I'm* the problem. I think they're the problem."

Arnie shook his head. "Men throw themselves at you! Who was that last guy? Raul?"

She thought about it. *Oh, yes. Raul.* With the empanadas. He showed up to her show, after about five weeks of ghosting her, with a warm plate of homemade empanadas. It was a super thoughtful gesture, but she was so confused about why she hadn't heard from him in so long. She had beaten herself up over what she may have done wrong and had come to terms with the fact that if someone didn't even want to text her back, then they weren't worth it. And then he showed up like that. Like nothing happened. Like she wouldn't be mad. It felt like the story of her life.

She felt like the only time she was given gifts by people she dated was as an apology. They gave a gift not for her, but for their own redemption. She had never sincerely been given flowers - and she loved flowers. She had received flowers twice, both times from someone she had broken up with trying to win her back. But it was too late. Why would flowers make her heart melt when they were still treating her shitty?

"Those empanadas were good, too," Arnie said. "Thanks for letting all the other comics eat them."

"Yeah, thanks for letting him know that's a weird thing

to do," Sophie said, referring to the fact that Raul sat down with Arnie at the bar after and wondered why Sophie wasn't overjoyed. She had thanked him, passed the plate around, and then went home with someone else. Arnie let him know that in the future, you have to actually talk to someone in order to build any kind of relationship.

But maybe, she wondered, she was missing something. Some patience or something. Should she have been overjoyed at the romantic gesture? Was that the rom com thing to do? Throw her arms around him and say "I've been waiting for you"!

She never felt like she had the time for all of that. She was too impatient, too convinced that there would be someone waiting around the bend to have unfulfilling sex with instead.

"That's what friends are for!" Arnie took another sip of his drink. He really was her best friend. She didn't consider herself very personable or social, so Arnie meant the world to her. They had met doing open mics six years ago when they were both figuring themselves out as comedians. Now they were strong performers and even stronger friends.

"But please know, Sophie. You are impossible."

That friendship meant that he had been around for every single dating disaster she has ever had. From crushes to hookups to breakups and more and he was no longer polite about her choices. She appreciated that. She was always worried about making mistakes that no one was calling her out for.

"That's not fair," she said. "It's not me. It's everyone else! Everyone I try to date is either boring or a total asshole. What am I supposed to do? Settle?"

"I think you just like to complain about everyone."

"Well. Everyone sucks."

"I rest my case." Arnie cleared his throat and gave her a look that said he had much more to say. It was a look she knew all too well. The look said *it's time for gossip.* "Did you know Matt is still talking about your breakup onstage?"

"Still?! He's still not over it?"

"Yeah, he's talking about it everywhere and going on podcasts and saying that his jokes are about a certain comedian back in Chicago."

"What a dick."

She rolled her eyes and finished off her drink. Arnie was looking at her intently, studying her face for any hints of negativity toward Matt. He was always doing that, always digging for more.

"Are you mad that he's successful?"

"Define success."

"A role in two movies, late night appearances, a special—"

"OH, those things? Hmmmm, let's see. Am I upset that my asshole ex-boyfriend has gained a lot of success since I broke up with him? Gee, I wonder."

"Me too. That's why I was asking!"

They laughed.

Matt was her ex-boyfriend and her only serious boyfriend. They had been together for almost two years and had even lived together, but it was always flawed. They were both comedians and the relationship was full of jealousy and comparisons, and lacking in sex. They simply didn't see eye-to-eye on so many things, including how much sex they should have. Matt told her that he didn't really care about sex, which was fine. Except that she did. She just wanted to have it a healthy amount and he could go weeks without it. It made her feel insecure, which was why his success was so bothersome. She had broken up with him, with this being a major reason, and he was going on about their horrible breakup. He was painting himself as a victim and she was being painted as a mean, crazy girlfriend.

She hated the reality that she had learned. Society

sexualizes women, but if women go after their own desires then they are crazy bitches. She couldn't tell everyone the truth: that he didn't like sex. That would emasculate him and make her seem like a nymphomaniac. It seemed so silly, but she felt like she couldn't. She couldn't make even one joke about it because all of her peers would know it was about him and it would get back to him. He'd be horrified. Just because she wasn't in love with him anymore didn't mean she wanted to tear him down. She still wanted him to be okay and she still felt that innate female desire to protect his feelings. Sometimes she hated herself for it.

The showroom had cleared out by this time, with only a few stragglers. One of them was fellow female comic Maura Simpson, a typical Logan Square hipster type. She had colorful tattoos draping her skinny arms and Warby Parker glasses that made her look cool and refined. Maura had plastered bright red lipstick on that contrasted with her jet black hair as she walked up to Arnie and Sophie and asked if she could sit down.

"Maura!" Arnie exclaimed, like she was family. He treated every comic this way. "I didn't know you were here."

"Yeah, I wanted to support the show. And you guys. But I didn't want to interrupt."

She gestured at the two of them in such a way that seemed to indicate...wait...did Maura think they were sleeping together? The idea was so silly to Sophie, who knew Arnie better than anyone and knew that he was gay.

Arnie got up wordlessly. When he walked toward the back of the room to find a bathroom, Maura leaned in. Sophie couldn't help but wonder why she continued to wear tanktops in the winter. It was Chicago. It was January. It was horrible outside. But then again, her tattoos were dazzling. She had a gorgeously intricate Phoenix on one arm rising from flames that spawned her entire bicep. On the other arm she wore charming daffodils. The difference between the two tattoos felt like they belonged to two different people.

"So how come you got to headline this show?" she asked.

Okay, hello to you, too. Sophie thought that, but didn't say it. Instead she shrugged. "Well, I was running late—"

"Really?"

"Yes. Why?"

Maura rolled her eyes. "Come on. You and Arnie obviously have a vibe."

"He's my best friend. And he's gay if that's what you mean—"

"I know, but like that even matters anymore. People hook up no matter what their sexuality is."

"Huh?"

"Is that how you got on this show?"

"This show? The one I do all the time?"

"Oh my God, don't play dumb with me, Sophie."

"I just want you to spell out what you're insinuating because it's so ridiculous."

"How is it ridiculous? I'd do it, too."

"Do what, Maura?!"

"Fuck Arnie to get on the show."

Sophie sighed. This was ridiculous. Some supportive female peer. She was tired of female comics trying to tear each other down and spreading the same archaic ideas that guys had about them. She didn't believe comedy was a competition the way everyone else seemed to. She didn't believe there was only room for so many women at the top. She thought there was space for everyone. And if not? Knock off a few guys to let the women have more room.

"Hear me out, Sophie. This is one of the most popular indie stand up shows in Chicago. I've been doing stand up longer than you and I still haven't been booked on this stupid show."

"Unreal."

Sophie grabbed her coat and buttoned it up just as Arnie was returning. He was surprised to see her go already, as he was in the mood for another round of drinks. Sophie wanted to get out of there and let Maura try whatever trick she was convinced that Sophie had done. *Go ahead and try to pick up, Arnie, you dumb bitch,* she thought as she wrapped a scarf around her neck.

"You leaving?" Arnie asked.

"Yup!"

"Hey, I'm sorry if I offended you—"

Arnie looked between them, wondering what could have possibly transpired in the two minutes he was away.

"No, you're not, Maura. And you know what? I'm glad that we female comics can stick together. So happy you have my back. Girl power!"

Sophie was dripping with so much sarcasm that it could have been collected into a bucket. As she stepped away from the bar, Maura slipped into her seat. It was up to her to deal with the confused Arnie who wanted to run after his best friend, although he knew he'd just text her later. Sophie had a habit of ghosting situations. She was a master of the French goodbye on the comedy scene. Sometimes she just wanted to be home alone. Well, with her roommate. But she usually kept to her own room.

A smiling young man with high cheekbones and deep brown eyes waved at her as she walked by. She smiled back.

"Hey!" he said, to grab her attention for a second longer. "You were great tonight. I don't mean to bother you. I just really liked your set."

"Oh, thank you for coming." Her standard response.

"I've seen you a few times. This was my favorite for sure."

She blushed.

"You're already leaving?" he asked.

"Well, it's a Monday night. I gotta go home and count my bathroom tiles."

He smiled wide at her. His smile felt like a wink. "Virgos know how to party."

How did he know she was a Virgo? She wanted to say that, but instead she said, "How did you know astrology is bullshit?"

He extended his hand for a shake. "I'm AJ."

"Sophie."

"I know. I've seen you perform before. Like...just now."

She giggled. He was cute.

"Would you want to get a drink with me? I'd love to pick your brain about comedy."

As a lifelong comedy nerd, that was her Achilles heel. If someone wanted to "pick her brain" that was likely all they'd find: comedy. She grinned and relented, going with AJ to the bar next door. That was the nice thing about Chicago - there was always another bar.

After a strong beer at Revolution Brewery, Sophie was definitely tipsy. She had never been much of a drinker, so she had no real tolerance. She got so drunk so quickly that she often wondered if she was allergic to alcohol. Regardless, she had drunkenly invited this darling man back to her apartment.

She didn't know much about AJ. AJ did a lot of the question asking. He let her drunkenly ramble on as he smiled and laughed. She loved that. She felt like the center of attention. He mentioned his day job in an office and that he had studied at Northwestern, but other than that she didn't know anything about him. Or was it Northeastern? Those were very different schools, but it didn't matter.

One thing she vaguely remembered him saying was that he was interested in comedy. He had mentioned going to some mics, but since she had never seen him before she didn't think he meant it. That might have made her a snob, but that was how she and countless comedians treated aspiring comics. There were people who said they did comedy like this guy, but who likely only went to an open mic one or two times. There were open mic-ers, people who seemed to live at open mics. They were either new at comedy and trying to get better or they were never going to get better. Either they were bad or they didn't want to challenge themselves, so they spent all their time at open mics bitterly wondering why they weren't booked on "real" shows. Then there were comedians. The ones who did comedy for real, for money, even if they only got paid $5 and a drink ticket good for a free beer at the bar. She was one of those.

She barely spent much time wondering about this guy's comedy or taking him seriously when he said that. He was too handsome to actually be *good* at comedy.

She was undressing him on her bed under the dim glow of a star-shaped paper lantern that hung above her bed. Her record player was playing Stevie Wonder, cause she thought maybe he'd think it was cool. She was embarrassed by her other records, which were mostly New Wave stuff handed down from her 80s hipster parents and folksy things she found at garage sales. This guy seemed kind of cool. He seemed like he might have money. She thought a guy like that would want some soul, that it might make him feel desirable.

It really didn't matter. Who cared what music was playing when you were hooking up?

The two of them had some fairly forgettable, tipsy sex. It was fine, the way that so many hookups were. The way that was forgettable. The way that Sophie would probably not count it in her "number". She was a grown woman approaching thirty. She didn't bother to count her sexual partners anymore. It wasn't high or anything, it just didn't matter. As long as she stayed safe, she could care less how many partners anyone had - including herself.

AJ was certainly attractive. After the deed, which barely took any time at all - not a thing she minded when it was as strange and mechanical as that had been - she traced her fingers along his smooth, golden chest.

He ran his fingers through her hair. She momentarily wondered if he had had fun. Then she wondered if that even mattered. She likely wouldn't see him again, so why dwell on whether or not he had a good time?

She could have asked, certainly. But she was never that good at being vulnerable and she wanted the power in a sexual situation like this. She loved control. She didn't want to relinquish it by seeming insecure or needy. Or by simply posing a question for him to answer. It was amazing how a woman offering her mind and heart could be seen as powerless. Power was in a woman's ability to shut the fuck up. She was the one who answered the questions, dealing out answers like tokens. She was cold suddenly and got up from the bed to change the record over.

"Man, Stevie Wonder. Classic," he said.

She figured. She turned it over, suddenly conscious of how naked she was in front of this guy she didn't know. He seemed comfortable on her bed. Oh God, was he going to spend the night?

She grabbed her robe, a thrift store kimono, from the hook on her closet door that was permanently open due to all the things she stuffed in there. The rest of her room was fairly clean, but that was because she got rid of messes by simply storing them in her closet.

She wrapped the kimono around herself and he sat up. He suddenly looked offended. Was it the kimono? She never considered it culturally insensitive, but—

"Why did you cover up?"

"I'm cold." She picked up her pants and debated putting them on. He watched her do this and asked her:

"You planning on going someplace?"

She smiled. But it was forced. Polite. This was the tricky part: getting him to leave. She knew she should have gone to his place even though it was all the way in the South Loop.

"This was fun! But I would appreciate just keeping this a one-time thing."

"How is it going to be a one-time thing? We're both comedians. We'll see each other."

She made a face. He immediately caught that. God, he was kind of quick.

"What's that?"

"Hm?"

"You made a face like what I said is ridiculous."

"I just feel like we don't have to broadcast this. Like, it happened, that's great. Let's move on."

"I'm not saying that—"

"Let's just keep this a one-time thing."

His face crinkled up. He seemed upset at the idea that this could be a casual hookup. Sophie didn't understand. Is that what men purported to want? "But it was fun. I'd like to do it again," he said.

"Yeah...I don't."

She knew she sounded cruel. She knew it was mean, but it made her feel powerful and she liked that. With her ex punching her on national TV, a moment of power after a hookup felt better than it probably should have.

"Why? What did I do wrong? I had fun—"

"Look, AJ, you *were* fun. You did nothing wrong. It's just that I didn't really know you were an aspiring comedian at first."

"Yeah, but I told you that on our way here—"

"Right, and I wanted to have sex with you, but I'm trying

not to get involved with any more comedians."

That may have sounded bad. She heard it as it was coming out of her mouth. "I wanted to have sex with you". God, she sounded like a frat boy.

"Okay…so you used me?"

"What? No—"

"You just said. You used me for sex."

"That's not what I meant."

She just really wasn't sure what she wanted. She wanted to have sex in the moment and so did he, so they did. She liked not feeling alone for the evening, but now she wanted to go to sleep by herself. She felt like spending the night was really intimate. She understood that didn't make a ton of sense considering he was just inside of her. But that's how she felt. The comfort and safety of sleep just felt too intimate to share with a stranger.

She could have absolutely said that, but that implied she wanted something special with him and she didn't think she did. She didn't really know the guy. And now that she was sobering up, she didn't want to fuck an open mic-er.

"Okay, AJ, I wanted to do this. But I really don't want any consequences from this. Got it?"

That sounded like a mafia threat which made her instantly wince at herself. *Girl, what are you saying? Abort this mission ASAP. Say whatever you can to get him to leave.*

"So you don't want a relationship is what you mean?"

"Yes! That. And—"

"You don't want me to talk about this onstage?"

Haha, that was cute. He acted like his act meant something or that he had an act at all. She didn't want him to feel bad or inferior to her, so she placated him.

"Exactly!"

"Okay, not a big deal." He smirked. "I respect you too much to talk about you onstage."

"Thanks, AJ. I am sorry I was being so weird."

"It's okay! Hey, I get it. You were insecure about me talking about you onstage like your ex or something."

"Oh, so you know Matt?"

"Everyone in comedy does. But don't worry. I won't."

"Thanks. And I'll do the same. I mean I know we're not on the same level, but still. I'd appreciate it."

That was the wrong thing to say. AJ's face scrunched. His oval eyes looked far away, stuck in a puzzle in his head. Now he was analyzing all of this, realizing what she may have really been saying all along.

"Not on the same level?" he asked. He sat up on the edge of the bed. He was still totally naked and she was wrapped in silk. She felt like an asshole on every inch of her body.

"I'm not saying you're not funny or whatever—"

"I'm very funny."

Oh, boy. Here we go. This man can't take the hit to his ego. How funny could this guy really be if Sophie had literally never heard of him or seen him before? The tables were turned and it didn't seem fair. This evening was now about her trying to soothe his hurt ego and make this guy who wasn't as talented or as accomplished as her feel better about himself. She had to nurture the baby bird back to health. This was why she didn't want to get involved with a young comedian. She really should have known better than to fuck an open mic-er.

"Totally!" she said in a positive tone that came off kind of condescending. "I'm sure all of your friends think you're super funny."

Jesus, Sophie, dig yourself out of this hole.

"And strangers, too," he said. "I've done Cole's Open Mic before. People like me."

"I know! That's not what I meant. What I meant is that you've been doing open mics for a few months maybe and I've been performing comedy for about seven years. Okay?

Now be a good boy and get the hell out of my apartment."

AJ stood up and put a shirt on, covering his fit figure from her and making it much easier to kick him out. He was no longer naked in her bed in a post-coital glow. He was now dressed and pissed at her. He got on his last bit of clothing and glared at her on his way out.

Alone in her apartment, she made a cup of tea in the kitchen. Chamomile lavender. Something calming to help her sleep. She brewed the leaves as she sang along to the Irma Thomas song playing on her roommate's record player in the living room. "Anyone Who Knows What Love Is". It was a sweet, powerful song.

Her roommate never used the record player and kept hers mostly as a status symbol. She had a total of six records prominently displayed on a small rack in the living room under the player she got from Urban Outfitters. Sometimes Sophie felt a little cooler than her. She had gotten hers at a thrift store when she was in high school, before records were cool for all millennials to have. Her parents had given their collection to her when they were trying to modernize. They thought it was cute their daughter got into enjoying music the way they did. She liked listening to the stuff her parents gave her. It made her feel nostalgic for Saturday mornings when her mom would play the B-52's or Prince or Depeche Mode and clean the house.

She sipped the tea that was still too hot to really drink, forcing the hot liquid onto the tip of her tongue, as she thought about her childhood for a moment, sitting in the chair and listening to Irma Thomas sing along to the sweet, fifties-style melody. She missed the simplicity of growing up, before she knew about one-night stands or what it felt like to bomb onstage.

"*If they tried love, they'd understand*," Irma effortlessly sang on the record.

She did love getting on stage though. There was nothing like making a room full of strangers fall in love with you for ten to fifteen minutes. It felt better than sex. Or at least better than being with a stranger for the night.

The music stopped. She sipped her tea, which was finally okay to drink. It was okay. This would all be okay.

FOUR

Sophie had an acting agent, but she didn't understand the point of having one anymore. Chicago wasn't nearly as big of a hub for acting opportunities as Los Angeles, or even New York, and yet she felt like she went on a million auditions. So then why didn't she ever book any? And how many more auditions were there really on the coasts?

Her agent sent her to a lot of commercial auditions where casting agents wanted someone "funny" to sell a super lame product that was nearly impossible to make funny. But they didn't want actual funny. They never did. What they really wanted was a smiling, energetic, attractive person to deliver a quirky line. They rarely wanted an actual comedian.

Still she would audition - for the hope of that huge paycheck - and then see those lines she said given to some super attractive actress in Hollywood when the commercial aired months later. She was on her way to an audition at Simon Casting when her phone rang. It was her agent, Tally Irvin, likely trying to pep her up before she read the sides for a grocery store commercial. She muted it as she opened the door and walked inside.

The nice intern working at the desk looked up at her

and smiled. She always wondered if the interns wanted to be agents or actors. Were they networking or trying to climb a corporate ladder? She could never make heads or tails of it, but she knew that they certainly did not want to be receptionists checking people into auditions. Either way, they almost all looked the same with huge stars in their eyes and a vague sense of importance for standing on the other side of a desk while hungry actors walked in.

"Hello! Are you here for the Fresh Market audition?"

God, that made her feel like a sellout.

"Yes! I'm Sophie Martin."

"Sophie..." she said as she checked the name off of her clipboard. "Wysocki or Martin?"

"Martin...who's Wysocki?"

The intern grinned as if Sophie made a joke. "Excellent. Here are the sides. Please take a seat and we'll call your name soon."

Sophie scanned the room. Four nervous actresses were sitting down, waiting for their turn. Maura was there. Great. Maura waved genuinely at Sophie. Really? After last night? Sophie figured Maura was just happy to know someone. Maura could be such a social climber and she didn't know the other actresses there, who were likely theater people.

Sophie always felt inadequate in these rooms. The other women looked like string beans. They all looked like they worshipped yoga and rode their bikes here, partially for fitness and environmental reasons, but mostly because they were poor. Acting was a hard industry. She always felt like she was cheating. As a comedian she didn't necessarily have to look a certain way. She didn't *have* to maintain a yoga instructor's body. And really - who had the time for that? Sophie could walk in and look like her short, size eight self. Size six on good days in July after the weather got nice and the Chicago winters weren't making her feel like she had to eat hot dogs for warmth.

Sophie sat down near Maura - leaving a seat in between them both. Maura eyed the seat like, "Are you serious?" but she didn't say anything about it. Finally, she leaned over the seat and said, "This is my first commercial audition."

"Really?"

Maura smiled anxiously. A perfect-looking woman sat across from them with evenly toned brown skin and curly hair that belonged in a hair magazine. She eyed them, sizing up her competition.

"Well. Word of advice?"

Maura looked at her expectedly, like Sophie really had advice. She had only ever booked one thing and it only aired in the south. She felt like she knew everything and nothing all at once, but that was show business. Nothing really made sense.

"They suck."

"Huh?"

"Commercial auditions. They suck. All of them." Sophie gestured sneakily at the woman across from them. "I bet she gets it."

"Shouldn't you, like, not say that in the waiting room?" Maura asked. "You're psyching people out. Or yourself. Or me. I'm not really sure what you're doing."

"I'm just telling the truth."

"With that defeatist attitude?"

A door opened. A peppy blonde who looked like she actually belonged in a startup's HR department came out with a clipboard. "Sophie Martin?"

"That's me!"

"Break a leg," Maura said flatly.

Sophie hardly heard her. She gathered her heavy winter coat and headshot and followed the kind woman into the room that only had a camera in front of a green screen. The woman took her spot behind the camera and pointed out the tape on the floor that Sophie would stand on. She looked overly dressed, almost like she felt the need to compete with the beautiful actors that came in all day. She looked up at Sophie with a blindingly white smile, a smile that was so kind it was suspicious. Prime conditions for an audition.

"Okay, Sophie, just slate your name and then read the copy for us directly into the camera."

"Will do. Any notes I should consider beforehand?"

She always asked this because she didn't know what to say. Was she supposed to ask questions? Was it like a job interview where you have to show that you're informed and interested? *Fresh Market is my favorite place to eat*! Or was it best to shut up and read the lines? She had no idea. She had an agent to help her comedy career, but she got strung into these gigs. She felt like she had been thrown into the deep end without a floatation device.

"Just have fun."

"Oh - you want me to have fun? That's asking a lot!"

The casting director stared blankly at her with her smile that was starting to feel creepy. It was a pleasant stare, but a stare that said she didn't understand sarcasm. Not at all.

"Whenever you're ready."

Sophie cleared her throat. She had kind of memorized the easy sides about Fresh Market. Usually, it didn't matter exactly what you said. She felt like they just wanted to see your energy and your face.

"New Year, new prices. Fresh Market has deals fit for a queen this 2018. So say *yas queen* to two-for-one bundles on chard! Or should we say '*yas chard?*'"

The casting director nodded, her blue eyes flickering behind the digital camera set up on a tripod.

"Okay! Very fun! I love it. But let's have more fun with it."

"More fun?"

"You know what I mean? Really let loose and have fun with the script."

Have fun with the script? This horrible script trying to sell chard? Sophie didn't totally know what she meant, so she just said the lines again with more enthusiasm. She tried exaggerating the "yas chard" part to sound as annoyingly millennial as she could.

The casting director stopped her - her smile never faltering. "Okay, you're, like, kind of just doing the script again."

"Right. But I'm trying to read it like I'm having fun. Like in a fun way."

The casting director nodded emphatically. "Okay, YES! Fun! We want that!"

"Cool! I thought you might."

"Yes, definitely!" She laughed. "Be fun, but just like... forget the script. But don't. You know what I mean. Go."

"...No."

"Hm?"

"I don't think I know what you mean," Sophie admitted.

She nodded. "Like these are words on a page and whatever! Like you can say them. Or you can say what Fresh Market means to you. What chard means to you."

"I mean, nothing. It means nothing. I'm reading the copy that some advertising dude was paid lots of money to write."

For once the casting director's smile dissipated. She pressed her lips together, keeping her blue eyes wide on Sophie as she considered the next piece of direction. Sophie truly had no idea where this was going. Did she want her to make up the commercial? Couldn't she just say that?

"Totally get what you're saying," the casting director said. "And, like, I SO get it. But, like, you can have fun with it."

She said that like she was granting Sophie permission to have fun. What exactly was fun? Now the casting director was starting to get in her head like a philosophy class. *Yes, but let's define fun. Can one truly ever have it?*

"Okay, straight up?" Sophie said, a bit exasperated. "By 'have fun with it' what do you mean? Do you mean improvise?"

Her face tightened up. She shook her head. "I didn't say that."

"Is that what you mean though? Do you want me to go off-script?"

Her eyes widened. It was like Sophie had just said "Macbeth" in a theater and now they were both cursed.

"Do you want me to improvise a new commercial just in case they want to use my jokes, but maybe not my face? Is that what you mean by fun?"

"Okay, I hear you, but I literally cannot say that I want you to improvise."

"What? Why?"

"I'm not technically allowed to. Do you understand? Like people wrote this and it's like...if you want to say this? Cool! But also you don't have to. Like just be you. Just be funny and fun—"

"So if I say something funny and catchy in this audition, will you guys just use it and not tell me? Or do I get writers' credit for it?"

The casting director's demeanor completely changed in that moment. Sophie had mentioned writing credits and she instantly turned the camera off. The smile was gone. She flatly looked at Sophie and said, "K. I think we got it."

"But I didn't have fun with it yet."

"No, that was good," she said without an iota of emotion. "That was fun. It felt SO fun."

The air was sucked out of the room and Sophie instantly felt crushed. She ruined it. Another opportunity that could have been booked was just thrown into the trash because Sophie just had to get mouthy.

Sophie was swiftly shooed out of the casting office and back into the waiting room. Maura looked at her with so much joy and excitement that Sophie suddenly felt like a monster for botching that audition. Why couldn't she have just smiled and said some stupid lines? What was wrong with her? She always had to poke a hole in the raft. She always had to let herself drown. This was why she wasn't as successful as Matt. She always got in her own stupid way while other people played along and got ahead.

Why can't I just play along?

"How'd it go?" Maura asked.

"Fine. Just have fun in there."

"It's fun?"

"A blast."

Sophie put on her coat and walked out the door as Maura's name was being called next.

She stepped outside onto 16th Street, Chicago's little film center that was complete with Cinespace and other small film studios and casting agencies. Chicago didn't have that big of a TV and film industry, but they were damn proud of what they had. The fact that it was small made Sophie feel both hopeful and depressed. If it was so small, shouldn't she be talented enough to make it? If she couldn't make it here, what made her think she could make it anywhere else?

She walked several blocks to wait for the bus back to her neighborhood in Logan Square. As she stood at the bus stop across from the huge, sprawling Douglas Park that was covered in winter sludge and browning snow, she noticed an ad at the bus stop. It was a Gap ad that had some comedians in it and then...was that...*Oh, Christ.* Her ex-boyfriend Matt was wearing a striped Gap sweater and a hat as he smiled dorkily. *Fuck.* She just bombed a stupid local grocery store commercial and Matt was doing national Gap ads that plastered his face all over the city. Fantastic.

Her phone rang. Tally. She had already dismissed the call earlier, so she picked it up.

"Sophie!" Tally said happily. Tally was always upbeat, but not in an annoying or fake way. She was as genuine as an agent could get. Sophie always felt like Tally was just doing her best and that she actually wanted her to do her best. She weirdly was one of the few people that Sophie trusted. "How did it go today?"

Sophie eyed the ad. There were Matt's hazel eyes, sparkling in a photo that was likely edited to bring out the greens in his eyes so they would pop against the colorful striped sweater. *Fuck it all.*

"Just the worst."

"Noooo. Come on, girl. I wanted that check."

Well, that was honest. So did Sophie.

"They did that thing I don't get where they want me to improvise—"

"We've talked about this! That's show biz code for 'make it up cause the copy sucks!'

"But I'm not a writer. I hate it when they want me to re-write the commercial for them!"

"What are you talking about? You write hilarious jokes all the time."

"But that's different."

Tally sighed on the line. Sophie could hear the distinct tap of a pen. She imagined Tally in her warm office sitting with her feet on her desk, tapping the pen on it impatiently as she considered letting Sophie go as a client.

"Okay, girl. It's been a hard month. Or two. Or four. Whatever. We'll pull it together."

"Yeah? You're not mad?" She felt so little and insecure asking that question. But she meant it. She felt like a child asking her mom to forgive her for doing a shitty job.

"Gotta be honest, you've been hard to book at certain

places."

She glanced at the ad again.

"Because of Matt?"

"Honestly? Yeah! Your ex-boyfriend did a lot of damage to your reputation. And people love him. Matt Kistler is funny; he sells tickets; he goes on TV; he delivers."

"So do I!"

She felt like the ad was watching her say that. She felt like Matt - the Matt she once lived with, the Matt who used to both encourage and discourage her - was watching her in that highly colorized ad. He was watching her and laughing to himself. She wondered if his oafish smile would turn into a smirk as she said that. She wondered if he would pop out of the ad and say, "No, you don't, love."

"But you're not famous," Tally said.

Well, he wasn't really either. That's what she wanted to say. But again - he was staring at her in a freaking bus ad.

"He's not famous-famous. He's just been on Colbert and in Netflix movies—"

"And he's in a Gap ad now. Have you seen it? I never considered him a print model, but I guess he's cute in a comedian way."

Sophie rolled her eyes. She looked away from the ad. She couldn't deal with imaginary Matt in the ad judging her as she got on the #52 bus to take her back to California and Milwaukee. He was somewhere in Hollywood, enjoying the palm trees and the sunshine. She was letting the dirty bus take her to her run-down Logan Square palace.

Sophie stepped on the bus and swiped her card. She was always scared she wouldn't have enough fare, so her heart stopped every time she swiped it. She was good to go. She walked to the back of the bus and took a seat. Everyone on the bus continued looking forward as if they were staring into their futures, staring into whatever bleak places the bus was taking everyone.

"What does any of this have to do with me?" Sophie asked Tally once she was seated.

"Cause he tells everyone that his jokes are about you! He's not coy about it at all."

"I wish I could sue him."

She wondered how much money he made now. Surely Netflix paid a handsome sum, even if he did just have bit parts in the movies.

"And kill your career? Good luck trying comedy when you're the not-famous ex who got revenge on her comedian boyfriend."

"Tally!"

"I'm just telling it like it is. I mean it feels like we have to do a PR campaign just to get you in certain bookers' good graces again. Like that dude at the Gallery Loft? He hates you."

The Gallery Loft was a small theater space that was known for letting comedians of all kinds try out anything there. It was above a dance studio and the huge, warm space was lit with twinkling Christmas lights. It was known for being an experimental playground for performers of all kinds and she used to perform there constantly when she and Matt were together. They ran a series of experimental shows that merged different kinds of comedy. Those were wonderful, rose-colored memories to look back on. It was insane that the owner would suddenly hate her.

"But the Gallery Loft guy used to love me!"

"Yeah, and he loved you and Matt together. Just get back together with the guy. It'll make my life so much easier. Yours, too."

"Whoa. You're my agent, not my matchmaker. Or my mom."

"I'm kidding! Kind of. It's been rough."

Suddenly Sophie felt responsibility toward her agent.

She had to make sure Tally knew it was going to be okay, that she had a good stake in her client and her friend.

"I'm fine. I'm doing Zanie's tonight. That's always a big crowd—"

"Yes! Okay, kill it!"

Sophie always loved it when Tally adopted the violent language used in the comedy community to describe doing well. You "kill". You "crush". You "destroy". You never just do well. It's always a massacre. And if it doesn't go well? You bomb. Lights out. You're finished.

"Kill it tonight and be as sweet as pie to everyone. Can you do that?"

"I'm not really a sweet person—"

"Right, but let's think PR overhaul on yourself."

"Fine. I'm America's sweetheart."

Tally laughed into the phone. "Oh, honey. We both know that's not true. But pretend to be! By the way, I'm having a party Friday night and you should definitely come."

Sophie groaned into the phone. A holiday party hosted by people-pleasing Tally Irvin? That felt like a nightmare. She didn't consider herself good at networking, which was an unfortunate skill that was necessary to succeed in that business. Just one of the many reasons Sophie felt herself stuck.

"I hate networking parties."

"There she is - America's sweetheart. K, see you Friday, Sophie."

Sophie hung up the phone and stared out the window, occasionally seeing Matt's ad strewn along bus stops throughout California Avenue until she safely arrived at her stop on Milwaukee Avenue. She was mad. She was disgusted. She was sad. But she found a way to direct all these feelings at herself. It wasn't Matt. It wasn't his success that was the problem. It was her lack of it.

FIVE

Zanies was a comedy institution in Chicago. And Nashville. And a few suburbs. It was one of those comedy club chains that popped up all over the place during the comedy boom. It had been in its Old Town location - just down the street from Second City - since the late seventies when it took over a building that was a former strip club. Only the finest entertainment in this old neighborhood!

Sophie loved the history of her city. She loved Chicago so much and always had, ever since she visited from the suburbs when she was a teenager. She would take the Metra train an hour and a half in from Joliet on the weekends to wander around the city. She loved walking downtown as a teenager and imagining herself as an adult hustling in the 9-to-5 grind in a tall skyscraper, holding a briefcase and wearing a blazer. Her actual adult life was much different. But she preferred it this way.

The Old Town neighborhood was once a bohemian mecca with cool artsy boutiques lining the streets and hippies assembling all over to plan protests. It was now filled with wealthy, older white people. The hippies had to get jobs and grow up eventually.

Sophie never knew what to expect when she performed at Zanies. Would it be stuffy neighborhood locals? Would it be tourists? Would it be foreigners who couldn't understand the jokes, but knew the rhythm of a joke and looked at her with careful smiles like they knew comedy was happening at them? It was always a crapshoot.

The building was a long, dark comedy club with its walls lined with the photos of comedy legends on the walls. Framed photos with names like Gilbert Gottfried and Chelsea Handler...and other that she never recognized. The headshots of so many hack comics and comedians that had likely quit ages ago still hung there. She would look at the big haired 80's comics with goofy smiles and huge shoulder pads and wonder what their current day job was. How many of these former comics were now writing calculator manuals?

She stared at these bygone victims of the comedy boom and wondered if she was next. Was she doomed to become another unknown face on these walls?

She walked straight to the back of the club to get to the green room, which was up a flight of stairs in the back. Fellow female comic Debra Mullen sat there writing in her notebook. She loved seeing Debra. One of her favorite things about her: no incessant talking. The two of them smiled warmly and exchanged pleasant 'Hello's before Debra went back to burying her face in her notebook. Sophie took hers out and placed her coat and bag on the ground - she never had that much reverence for her things - as she sat down beside Debra. Bliss.

After only seconds of silence, Debra said, "I can't believe they are letting two women co-feature on one show."

"For a male headliner no less!"

"Seems dubious to me," she said and went back to her notebook.

Sophie hadn't thought of it like that previously. She and

Debra had both been asked to co-feature, which meant they would each do about fifteen minutes of comedy, before the guy whose face was on the bill closed out the show. He was some hack road comic that Sophie had never actually heard of. She had googled a video of his comedy and turned it off after two minutes. She wondered if his crowd would actually be into her comedy. Or Debra's, for that matter. So then why both of them on one show?

Glenn, the owner of the club, walked out of his office to greet them. Wearing tinted glasses on his round face, he smiled, baring two sharp canines that legitimately looked like fangs, like he was the Vampire of Old Town, sucking the life out of hopeful young comics desperate for stage time.

"Okay, we have everybody here. Show starts in ten," he said, clapping his hands together.

"Thank you, Glenn," Debra said without really looking up.

"Thank you!" Sophie said, giving him a full smile. She was slightly more of a people-pleaser than Debra.

Glenn stared down at them in horror. The two of them were practically matching - both wearing dark colored turtlenecks.

Then he said, "Whoa, sweetie, you're wearing that onstage?"

She looked down at her outfit. She heard Debra mouth "Sweetie" as she eyed her own slouchy black turtleneck and jeans ensemble carefully. Her hair was up in a bun. She wore her berry colored lipstick and mascara. She had her grandmother's ring on her right ring finger, a silver and amethyst beauty that made her feel powerful when wearing it, as if she was harnessing ancestral powers. She had 90's hoop earrings that she'd snagged from the vintage store she worked part time in. She didn't see what was wrong with this look. It was chic. It was hip. It was also good enough for a

Chicago winter.

"Are you in mourning?"

"It's cold outside."

"Christ, Sophie," Glenn said, as if Sophie had turned up in blackface. "I booked you for the sex appeal."

"Oh," she said. Because that was all she could say in that moment. It didn't seem real, or...legal. "But you've seen me perform before, right?"

"I mean, I don't know—"

"I pretty much always wear this."

"There aren't sexy comics, Glenn," Debra chimed in, and she was right. The idea of a sexy comic seemed ridiculous. Maybe sex appeal worked for the movies or something, but for comedy? Most female comedians would be laughed out of town if they tried to be legitimately hot onstage. Women had to ride a thin line to get the respect of their peers and the respect of the audience.

"The headliner likes hot young women to open for him," Glenn said, somewhat apologetically. He threw his hands up, like he was surrendering to these two women. "That's why I booked you."

"Gee, I could take my shirt off," Debra said. "I've got a nice bra on underneath this. It's worth the price of admission."

"No, not you, Deb! You're too...I meant Sophie. She's got that whole ethnically ambiguous look."

Debra rolled her eyes and went back to her joke book. Glenn was being insanely insulting to them.

"And here I thought you booked me for my talent," Sophie said.

It was always discouraging in comedy to be reminded of being a woman and thus of being less than. The sex appeal thing didn't make sense. That was never what she was really going for. She rarely dressed in revealing ways. She only kind of talked about sexual encounters onstage. So this was just because she was kind of cute? And why didn't this count for Debra?

"You're the hot girl on the line-up! I've got you and the mino chick. Come on, girls. What are you missing?"

"Mino?" Debra asked, having not realized she met a specification, too.

"Minority."

"You just said you liked Sophie for being Spanish or whatever - what are you?"

"Half Cuban."

"That counts," Debra said. She knew what he meant. She wanted to hear him say it.

He was wildly uncomfortable by the conversation - far more than by the sexy one. His pink cheeks got red and he threw up his hands again. "Minority. Ethnic. Whatever you want to call it. You're the black girl on the lineup."

"Who is also hot? What is this, Glenn?"

Debra put her face back down in her notebook. Glenn wasn't bothered by their discomfort. He truly didn't think he was doing anything wrong.

"I'm moving our club to the new age. People keep bugging me, saying we don't book women and minorities—"

"Well, you don't," Debra said. "You book white men."

"And I'm changing that."

"With this one show?" Sophie asked.

"You should take it as a compliment! The headliner saw your headshot and wanted you. He picked you out of like five other local girls."

"Ew, just from my headshot? He didn't watch my clip?"

Glenn shrugged as if to say *What are you gonna do?* He refused to admit what could be insulting about any of this. The headliner chose her *face*. He didn't give a shit about what her jokes were like.

"Glenn, I'm not conventionally hot," Sophie said, feeling

self-conscious about being a piece of meat onstage.

"Who cares? This is Chicago, babe. While you may not even be on the scale in LA, you're like a Chicago 8. Hell, you're a Montana 15."

Glenn disappeared for a second to rummage through a box labeled "costumes". Why did this old comedy club have a costume box? He finally pulled out a slinky red velvet dress that looked like a Santa costume. It was basically velvet lingerie made for a December burlesque show.

"You're wearing this."

Glenn tossed the piece of clothing to Sophie and stormed out.

"Mino," Debra said. "That has a nice ring to it. I think I'll name my first born Mino."

Sophie went into the bathroom to put on that teeny tiny piece of clothing. When held in her hands, she didn't see how it would possibly fit her. She slipped it on, and the "dress" barely stretched over her ass. She was terrified the white fur trip at the bottom would ride up her booty as she stepped onto the stage. She felt grateful that she was wearing silk undies and not the period-stained cotton ones that she typically wore on a casual day. The spandex-like velvet stuck to her body, stretching tightly over her tummy. She felt *so* insecure. To top it all off, there were built-in bra cups to push up her cleavage and let the audience get a boner from comedian Mrs. Claus.

When she walked out of the bathroom in her ridiculous costume, Debra took one look at her and burst into guffaws.

"There's no way you're really doing this, is there?" she asked, making Sophie feel even more idiotic than she already felt.

It hadn't occurred to Sophie to say no. She was so scared that if she refused he would say she couldn't perform there again, no matter how loudly she told this ridiculous story.

She needed the paycheck. She wanted the money, the credit, and respect of her community of comedians. She wanted to do the show and if this was the stipulation...she suppose she had to do this stupid gimmick.

"You can say no," Debra said. "Go home."

Say no...and let Debra have her money and time? She never knew if a comedian actually had her back or was looking out for themselves. She decided to tough it out and do the show.

"I need the money," Sophie told her before leaving the green room. "Besides, it's humbling for a hot girl like myself to wear something so truly unflattering!"

She was, of course, the comic to kick off the show. A pink-faced guy she didn't know was hosting and asked the audience to give it up for their next comedian, Sophie Martin.

She stepped carefully up the stairs to the stage - in the same slip-on loafers that she had worn there - trying to pull down on the white trim of her dress as she walked up. She felt so impossibly naked up there. The lights had never felt brighter. Her skin had never felt colder. She had never felt more exposed. She may as well have been naked, because that was how it felt.

Sophie approached the microphone - it always smelled like B.O. at Zanie's. She didn't think they had cleaned it or replaced it since the 80's. It smelled like countless comics' bad breath and anxiety. So many horrible jokes' stink bombed straight into that microphone and there she was, feeling like she was about to do the same.

She grabbed the mic and took it off the stand. "Yes! Give it up for me," she said to the audience that was clapping and taking her all in. "This is just what I wear every day."

The audience laughed. That was usually all it took to let her know she would okay. She sometimes got nervous before her sets, but it always faded away when the audience reacted well to her opening lines. Sometimes it was a rough start that felt like running uphill, but other times it felt as smooth as a toboggan ride. This was going to be a weird one, but she knew if she just made several jokes about her little red getup at the top, then the audience would be on board. In fact, why not tell them the story? Why not be her honest self for once? She was always concerned about protecting people's feelings, but Glenn clearly didn't give a shit about her feelings when he dressed her up like a sex doll for the stage. This place used to be a strip club, but it wasn't anymore. It was 2018. Women were allowed to be clothed and funny onstage.

"Wanna know why I'm dressed this way?" she asked.

"Hell yeah!" a guy shouted from the back. The audience laughed at him and started wooing. Oh, no. This might not go as well as she had thought. Sometimes comedy felt like a tug-of-war with the audience, particularly when there was an unruly audience member. If the audience sided with the heckler, they pulled the rope and left the comic on their ass, struggling to get back on their feet and take control of the situation.

The rest of the set was a bit of a nightmare. This "sex appeal" thing wasn't working. The audience didn't want to hear her jokes about weird stuff her dad says or dating a vegetarian. They didn't want to know about her high school reunion. They just wanted to yell about the fact that they could see every inch of her body.

After the show Debra and Sophie immediately bolted for Debra's car. They decided not to stay for the whole headliner after their performances. They didn't care about that dude and after the way Glenn had treated them before the show, they didn't feel like caring about any old-school male comic. They both silently left the building and didn't say a word until they were safely seated in Debra's sedan.

"What a shit show that was!" Sophie said when she was finally able to.

"No kidding. That crowd wasn't ready for me after ogling your Lil' Miss Claus get up."

"They also didn't want to hear my normal jokes nearly as much as me talking about the stupid costume. Sorry that didn't set you up well."

"No worries. You're the one who isn't going to get booked there again."

"Do you think so?" Sophie asked earnestly, before remembering that Glenn was being a sexist and racist piece of shit. "Ugh, I messed up and now Glenn thinks I'm not funny."

"Who cares what Glenn thinks? Honestly, I'm shocked you went along with all that."

Sophie got red in her cheeks. She was shocked she did, too. She thought she was stronger than that, more feminist. And yet when push came to shove, she got shoved onstage in a slutty costume.

"He's an old, out-of-touch white dude who thinks Carrot Top is underrated," Debra was saying. "You care too much about what people think."

"At least I looked good."

"Yeah, you should have just sung 'Happy Birthday, Mr. President.'" Debra then did her best Marilyn Monroe impression, talking like an airy baby whose hair bleach just infected their adult brain. "I can't possibly tell jokes, Mr. President. My bosom will get in the way!"

They pulled away to head to Cole's Bar for the popular Wednesday night open mic. They thought perhaps an open mic with their peers - dressed in their normal clothes - would be a good palate cleanser from that disaster.

When they got to Cole's, it was already packed, which was pretty typical. This dive bar with a pool table and a performance space behind a curtain in the back was the place to be for its cheap drinks, friendly bartender, and good comedy. It wasn't uncommon for a celebrity comic to drop in and do a set. Whenever that happened the back room filled with local hipsters trying to get a pic for Instagram. The unlucky comic that followed the stunning celeb comedian always had to tell their jokes to the backs of people leaving the back room in order to approach the comedian who was just on stage and now hanging out at the bar. It was a common occurrence there, which was why the place tended to be so popular. It was an open mic, but it was attended as if it were a popular show. A free show with sometimes horrendous comedy.

Debra and Sophie made their way to the back, nodding and smiling to several thirsty and bitter comedians they recognized on their way. When they opened the curtain to the back room, they found Arnie leaning against the wall with his arms folded.

"Debra! Haven't seen you in a while," he whispered excitedly as he gave her a side hug.

"I need a hug, too, Arnie," Sophie said. "I just shat the bed at Zanie's."

"This is our palate cleanser," Debra affirmed.

Arnie's face twisted into disgust. "Oh, my God. And you guys came to an open mic? What are you thinking? Go get ice cream. Go do anything else."

"What's wrong with an open mic?" Debra asked sincerely.

"Everything," Arnie said.

They turned their attention to the skinny twenty-one boy year old struggling with his material on stage. The lights washed out his winter-pale complexion and made him squint at the notebook where his genius was written. Those jokes never seemed as genius when you were actually on stage saying them to silence. It felt like a black hole when you bombed at Cole's. Your words were being sucked into the dark, crowded room that stared back at you as if you were an alien. *Why would you say these jokes to us?* It felt like the audience was saying back in their silence. *What made you think we would want this?*

But when it was successful? It felt like you were a preacher delivering a sermon on salvation and everyone was begging to be saved. That was comedy, though. Two sides of the same validation-seeking coin.

The host, a commanding female comic who knew how to take control of the stage after a comic bombed, gracefully led the young man off. She asked the audience to clap for him as if he hadn't just delivered four minutes of silence.

"All right! Give it up for the last guy, huh?" she asked with a smile. God, she had to do this all night. What a trooper. "We have a new face here next. I haven't seen this guy here before, so you know what to do. Give him a big Cole's welcome. Put your hands together for AJ Tran."

Sophie's face fell.

"No. Oh, no."

AJ, the man she had hooked up with only days ago, took the stage. That beautiful smile she remembered from the other day had morphed into a look of pure intensity and anger. He took the mic, shook the host's hand, and looked out into the crowd. He found Sophie. He frowned at her from the stage with fury in his eyes.

"Did he just look at you?" Debra asked.

"I may have done something I regret the other night."

"Noooooo!" Arnie said, loud enough for the people around them to hear. He got several looks from uppity hipsters with cool dyed hair, piercings, and white-framed glasses that made them all look like disco queens.

"Sophie! An open mic-er?!" Debra whispered to her. "Are you insane?"

"I know—"

Ted cleared his throat and finally brought the mic to his chest. He shouted, "You all know Sophie Martin?"

Just like that, everyone in the room who did know her turned to glance at her. The room got subsequently silent.

"Well, she's a fucking bitch, and here's why."

The room reacted in various ways. Some people gasped, some cheered him on with a clap - probably not realizing she was a real person who was in the room - some people whispered to each other to say 'I do know her' or 'isn't she a comedian?' or 'isn't she right there?' Sophie felt her intestines twist and drop inside of her. Ted even glanced at her to see her reaction before glancing back at the people sitting at the cabaret tables in front of the stage.

"I don't care! I'll say it!"

Arnie grabbed Sophie's arm and pulled her toward him. "Dude. What did you do?"

"I didn't realize I was playing with fire when I hooked up with this guy. He seemed like a harmless, regular dude."

"She told me she wanted to keep us secret. Not do it again. Like what? She's some kind of prize? I mean, yeah, I've had a crush on her for months—"

Sophie leaned into her friends, but whispered loud enough for the people around her to hear just in case they knew it was her. "I didn't even know who he was!"

"But she said we aren't on the same level. Yeah. Can you believe that?"

Groans from the crowd. Christ.

"I'm so sorry, your majesty. Shall I get a ladder so that I can be worthy of making eye contact with you?"

The host approached Sophie like a quiet, determined animal, and whispered urgently, "Do you want to go next?" She could sense the good theater that would create.

"I don't know," Sophie said. "What should I do?"

The host shrugged. "Go after him. It's what I would do."

Sophie had never been a comedy-as-revenge kind of person. She was afraid of hurting someone's feelings or making a bigger mess of herself. Her mother had always taught her to "kill 'em with kindness" and be the bigger person by walking away. Sometimes she feared that this attitude was what held her back in comedy.

"Hey, maybe we should get out of here?" Debra suggested. "Ice cream sounds good right about now."

"Yeah, that's a good idea," Arnie said. "Get her out of here, Debra. It isn't good for my career to be seen around her right now."

"Gee, thanks, pal," Sophie said.

"Suit yourself," the host said. "Arnie, you're next, then!"

"Yeah, and I'm not touching this with a ten-foot pole. Bye, ladies!"

As Debra and Sophie made their way to the exit, they could still hear AJ swearing about her. He saw her leaving - great. There was no way he wasn't going to mention that.

"She's leaving during my set. What's wrong? Too real? Guess I don't need to be some sadsack comedian stuck in Chicago for like ten years or whatever." Ted laughed into the mic. People were reacting to his fervor and wooing at his fearlessness at going after his bad hookup. He certainly colored it to make him look more pathetic. The crush on her? What the fuck was that? Sophie felt like she was two feet tall inside, but outside she was a ten-foot giant that couldn't get out of the building without getting noticed fast enough.

AJ pounded his chest like he was a hero. "I'm the real thing, baby. Woo! I'm gonna be famous!"

Arnie shook his head, still watching this trainwreck. Then he said, to no one in particular, "Woof. Tell a joke, kid."

Sophie held in her fury until she and Debra got outside.

They walked up the street a little ways, Debra watching her carefully as if trying to steady herself before a bomb went off, before Sophie finally shouted: "What the actual fuck?!"

"Honestly? Bravo, girl! I have not seen a young white man get that upset over pussy in a while. I thought I was too old to see such a tantrum."

"God, I fucked up. Did I? Did I fuck up?"

Debra shrugged and nodded as if to say *well, yeah*. Sophie groaned.

Debra, who was not much of a hugger, patted Sophie on the shoulder affectionately and pityingly.

"Honestly, Sophie? Between your famous and creepy ex and that crybaby in there - how do you ever get onstage?"

Sophie looked at her in distress. She didn't know how to answer the question. It was the same thing her agent wondered, the same thing she wondered. The anxiety was swimming in her stomach making her feel like she might wretch.

"It's ridiculous, isn't it?"

"You're making me grateful I don't sleep with comedians. Yikes."

"Ugh, I didn't mean to! I don't want to sleep with the dude again and he gets to go up and talk shit about me?"

"First lesson: Never sleep with anyone younger than you." She then paused for a moment and added, "In comedy."

"It's just...I'm tired of these guys getting to say what they want." Sophie felt herself saying these things half-tearfully, which scared her. She was scared of showing too much emotion over these dumb guys and of scaring away Debra's consolation. She didn't want Debra to think she was weak, or petty, or...there she was, caring what other people thought again. Fuck it. She was going to get angry. She had the right to be.

"It's frustrating because he's an angry guy with a

microphone so everyone has to listen. Just like Matt. When I'm angry on the mic, they tune it out."

"Have you ever tried to do that? Get angry about some guy on the mic?"

"No...I kind of want to, but I feel too polite and protective or whatever to do it. Have you?"

Debra shook her head. "But can you imagine if we did?"

"That's the thing! I feel like it's expected that I won't complain about this or anything else and if I do I'm being a bitch."

"OR not taking the joke."

Sophie leaned against the wall of the taco restaurant down the street from Cole's. A few people were leaving the bar, smoking cigarettes as they walked by, and looked at her knowing it was the girl that AJ was talking about. A neon-haired couple couldn't stop looking at her. She flipped them off as they went by.

"At least you're white," Debra said as a bit of solace.

"I'm half-Cuban—"

"Bitch, whatever. You look Italian. What I'm saying is that it would be slightly easier for you to get up there and rail on those guys than me. No one likes an angry black woman. I feel like they don't even listen to what we say half the time."

Sophie nodded. Debra had a point that was hard to argue with. It was just true. Sophie couldn't think of anything to say, except, "What a weird life we've chosen to live."

Debra leaned against the wall with her, then said wistfully, "But I love it. Couldn't imagine doing anything else."

"That and I have no real skills."

"No, you really don't," Debra laughed.

SIX

It was pretty rare that Sophie was able to convince herself to leave the house and venture out of her neighborhood on a night off, especially when it was cold. But it was a Friday night and she didn't have a show, so she put on a saucy little party dress that made her feel cute. She usually felt like a poor comic in the old clothes she'd had since college. She put on the emerald green wrap dress her own mother had given her last Christmas as an effort to boost her daughter's wardrobe.

"You're almost thirty," her mother had told her then 28 years old daughter. "You have to dress like it. Besides, this is why you date losers. You are attracting them to you!"

She was dressed to impress and talked herself up to network on her way over. She loved watching people who were delightful at parties and found herself envious that that wasn't her. She wasn't the one giving hugs and telling stories with wide, open-mouthed smiles. The kinds of smiles that were always mid-laugh. The kinds of smiles that people wanted to be around like a fire in the cold. She wanted to be the kind of person who radiated heat. But, as she arrived to Tally's North Center apartment on a quiet street off of Lincoln Avenue, she could feel all her ideas of warmth dissipate. She wasn't that person. She could turn on the charm onstage, but off stage she always felt tired. She felt too serious, too critical, too everything bad. Perhaps she was just too insecure.

No, you can do this, she thought to herself as she reached for her phone to double-check the address. She stood outside of the brick three-flat building that Tally lived in and could hear people crowding the second floor. They were all up there, being warm, being funny. She wanted to go home and watch movies in her bed.

Parties are fun. Parties are good. People like parties. You like people. Oh, my God, no you don't—

"Sophie! You made it!"

It was too late for her to go home. The door swung open and Tally greeted her, putting an arm around her. Tally wore an elegant-looking maxi dress that had that bohemian look of 'oh this? It's nothing. I got it on sale, I swear' while simultaneously looking like it cost $300. She wondered in that instant how much money her agent made. She didn't live in the ritziest building or neighborhood. It was all just nice. But she definitely looked expensive.

"You look fantastic, Tally."

"Oh this? It's nothing." Sophie raised an eyebrow. "It isn't too extra, right? I thought it was pretty casual-cool. Like, still good for a party. Oh, who cares. A hostess has to dress the part, right?"

She followed Tally up to the second floor while Tally rattled off the names of people who were inside that she had to meet. They opened the door to the apartment on the second floor to find people everywhere. Wow, Tally knew a lot of people. And Sophie didn't know any of them.

For a second she felt overwhelming panic. She wanted so badly to turn around and ghost this place. Maybe she should just run to a Golden Nugget and hide her party shame in a plate of nighttime scrambled eggs.

Tally ran off with her coat somewhere that Sophie couldn't see. People seemed to know each other as everyone was paired off into small groups that had a lot of laughter and discussion. Suddenly Sophie heard Tally shouting her name. She followed the noise into the kitchen, where Tally was standing near the refrigerator, talking to a man she didn't know. He was dressed in a burgundy sweater that seemed too big for his body and wore oval glasses on his long face. He smiled shyly at Sophie as she came near.

"Sophie, this is Fred. Fred, Sophie."

They shook hands as Tally stood by, proudly watching. She had no idea why she was being made to meet this person.

"I've never met a Fred I didn't like!" Sophie said. "Well, I've only known one Fred. I went to college with him. He used to wear a cape."

"I knew I was forgetting something," Fred said. His voice was soft, but confident. It made her smile.

"Sophie is a stand-up comedian," Tally offered as if that was actually impressive to anyone. "You guys would get along great!"

Sophie turned back to him. He was dressed as poorly as a comedian, she supposed, but only because the sweater didn't fit right. The sweater actually looked really nice. He was clean-shaven and had an even olive tone. He didn't look tired or bloated. No, he didn't look like a standup comedian.

"Are you a comedian?" Sophie asked him.

He blushed. Why was he blushing? Maybe she made him nervous. He quietly said, "Um, no. Not really. Well, I'm a writer."

"Oh! What kind of writing?"

"Humor. I write for The Onion."

Sophie's face tightened a little. That was an elusive job that she had, of course, wanted. She never knew how to get it. When she was a teenager riding the Metra train into the city, she would always pick up a paper copy of The Onion downtown. She'd read it on the way back home and wonder how she could write for them someday. It seemed like a dream. Now that she was an adult comedian living in Chicago, where they were headquartered, she would occasionally meet a writer and would be overcome with envy and discouragement. Envy, obviously, because she wanted that position. Discouragement because every writer she had ever met was an Ivy League white person, typically male.

She was constantly upset that that was the unwritten rule in comedy. Do you want the big jobs? Well, let's hope you are from a good family that could afford to send you to Princeton and it helps if you can be one-of-the-boys. Oh, but *trust us,* we're looking for diversity - *wink wink!*

"Be right back, guys," Tally said. She looked delighting, like she had just performed an excellent matchmaking job. "You two chat."

"The Onion?" Sophie was trying to hide her bitterness. "That's cool. You're like a big writer boy?"

Fred bashfully nodded. He didn't seem like the other writers she had met. He seemed really quiet and humble. He didn't act as if he knew he was the funniest person in the room.

"Yeah, I'm a big boy. I've only had the job for a few months. It's why I moved to Chicago."

"Where did you move from?"

"New York."

"Oh, I thought I sensed an air of superiority."

"It wafts off of me along with the scent of a proper pizza."

"Hey! Don't you say anything bad about Chicago pizza."

She liked him. He was quick…and he felt the same way about her.

"New York is just where I went to college," he said. "I promise I'm not all bad."

Did she detect a slight accent? He sounded vaguely foreign, like Madonna did when she was married to Guy Richie. It could just be a fancy-boy affectation, as if living in New York and writing for a prestigious comedy rag wasn't impressive enough.

"Where are you from, then?" she asked him.

"Montreal."

"Oh! You're *Canadian*!" she said that as if it explained why he was so quiet and nice. It did explain the very faint accent she heard from North America's Europe. She didn't finish saying anything else and instead just stared at him with wide eyes. He stared back inquisitively for a moment. Finally, he asked her, "You're a Chicago girl then?"

"Born and raised. I taste like Malort and Portillo's. Hey, is there any food here?"

Fred pointed to a large table with an impressive spread of food that was in the next room. How could she have missed a beautiful display like that?

"The food seems unmanned," Fred said. "Shall we?"

Sophie led the way and the two of them hovered over the table like hungry raccoons about to dig into a garbage can feast. Only this wasn't garbage. These were snacks of all kinds, from crostini to cheese cubes to salami to cookies. They both began to pick at the food like they were starving.

"So, Fred from Montreal—"

"It's actually Frederic," he said with a French twinge.

"Oh! How did you know what I was going—"

"Every American is always like 'a French Canadian named Fred? That is suspicious'."

"So. The Onion? Um...how did that happen?"

Fred laughed awkwardly. She was used to kind of being brash and forward with her fellow comics and guys in general. She now realized she was around someone ostensibly more successful than her and she had just asked the loathed 'how did you get that' question. She felt like a doofus, so she attempted to cover it up.

"I'm so sorry. Is that a weird thing to ask? I'm genuinely curious—"

"From some people it could be kind of gauche, but from you? I'll let it slide."

At least she wasn't "some people".

"I know it's awkward, though," Sophie said, to really hit home that she was somehow different than the vague others he was referring to. "I hate when people ask me stuff like that."

"So much of comedy and writing is so nebulous. You have to ask or you'll never know."

At that same moment Sophie had jammed too many chips into her mouth at once. She bit down hard and the crunch of chips spattered out of her mouth and onto her own cute party dress. A teeny triangle of chip fell onto Fred's sweater. It was very unladylike. Very gauche.

"Are you sure you're a comedian? Because you seem like a model."

She wiped the crumbs away from her mouth and smiled a very chippy and toothy smile.

"My secret? I'm both!"

They both laughed. She felt good making him laugh. It was like she was scoring points in some kind of comedy game. *Oh, you think you're more important than me because you get regularly paid to write for one of the most lauded comedy institutions in the country? Well, take that. I just made you laugh by shattering chips out of my mouth!*

"Actually, I get told that a lot."

"What? That people think you are a model?"

"No, but, like, people tell me I'm too pretty to be a comedian sometimes. Okay, I know it sounds vain, but I swear to you. Like a month ago I met a random old lady who asked what I did and when I told her she shook her head. Like she was my grandma or something! She told me I was too pretty to debase myself as a comedian."

At that moment Fred could have flirted with her by saying something like, 'she wasn't wrong' or 'well, you are really pretty'. Sophie wondered if he would say something like that. She wondered if he thought she was pretty at all. Maybe he was listening to this story and thinking, 'what are you talking about?'

“Aw, she was flirting with you,” he said, in a joking and not very flirtatious way. It made Sophie a little embarrassed. She shouldn’t have sounded so vain. It didn’t matter if it had happened. Maybe she wasn’t actually that pretty at all. She looked at the bowl of chips she had been jamming her hand in and felt an intense self-hatred. She wished she could leave her body just so that she could slap herself in the face.

Luckily, Tally interrupted the self-loathing when she fluttered up to the two of them like a beautiful butterfly in a panic.

“So sorry, Sophie, but Matt is here.”

Sophie looked around instinctively. She didn’t immediately see him. Until her eyes landed on his impossibly tall, broad figure wearing the classic plaid shirt typical of many comedians. She wanted to punch him in his stupid, newly-tanned-from-a-life-in-Hollywood face.

“Wait. Why did you invite him—”

“I didn’t. Apparently I invited his girlfriend.”

This was news to Sophie.

“Girlfriend?”

“I had no idea they were together.”

“He has a fucking girlfriend?”

Fred was still standing in the middle of all of this, his eyes darting between the two of them as he attempted to quietly make sense of what was happening.

“Recent ex or...?”

“No. Not recent. But that scumbag’s been acting like he’s still desperately heartbroken.”

“Yeah, thus the secret girlfriend.”

“He’s been going around town - going on shows and podcasts, going on fucking TV - playing victim, telling jokes about me, and now I learn that he has a girlfriend. What the fuck?”

“Okay, I truly didn’t know. I didn’t know he was in town!

So this is not my fault."

Fred shrugged and said, "It could be his date?"

Sophie looked at him like *'are you out of your mind?'*

"Or it could not be that thing I just said," he said as a bit of an apology for suggesting such a stupid thing about a situation that he knew nothing about.

"So she introduced him to me as boyfriend and I was like 'oh, awkward'. I know Matt. Who doesn't?"

"I don't," Fred said.

Sophie overrode them all as if no one had said anything. Her eyes were laser-focused on that dumb bumbling asshole who was still standing by the door smiling at people. She wondered if the slender, ethnically ambiguous woman beside him was his girlfriend. She was gorgeous, of course. Of course he had to have a hot piece of arm candy to tote around Chicago whenever he came back. She was one of those cool girls who had a shaved head because she was too beautiful for hair. She had huge hoop earrings and natural-looking makeup that highlighted her shimmering face. Or maybe the makeup made her face shimmer. Either way she was doing the thing that Sophie was envious of. She was being a glittering beacon of light and Matt had flown to her for warmth. Unbelievable.

She was not mad at either of them. She wasn't necessarily jealous, other than being jealous of this woman's fit figure that she showed off in a skin-tight jumpsuit. A jumpsuit. Who the fuck is actually able to pull off a jumpsuit without looking like a clown? No one normal, anyway. Only celebrities. Only models.

She was mad in that way that you often get about an ex's choices. She knew him so well and was infuriated that with his newfound success he had to do the asshole thing of having the hottest possible girlfriend. He had to show up at his ex's agent's house and act like it wasn't a big deal. She knew him well enough to know he had an inkling she would be there.

He wanted her to see him...but he also likely didn't want Sophie to confront him about the career hell she had been through on account of him. Having a slightly more famous ex-boyfriend was enough of a sting. Having that guy get famous off of jokes made about you? That really fucking hurt.

"This fucking asshole. He's had a girlfriend this whole time."

Sophie shoved her food plate at Fred who grabbed it just before it fell out of his hands. Tally was nervous about this. She didn't want drama at her party. She followed Sophie as she made her way over to Matt and his graceful-looking girlfriend.

"Sophie, wait—" Tally was saying behind her. But it was too late. Her eyes zeroed in on Matt like a missile locked and loaded. Matt looked over, feeling the target on him, and his face dropped.

"Sophie."

"Dog fucker."

Matt's arm candy was outraged on his behalf. "Who are you—"

"Don't worry about it, Viv," he said. "This is Sophie."

"Oh, yeah, I'm sure she knows all about me. The world knows about me, Matt. And things I didn't know about me. Some fun little lies you cooked up. Like lies about me cheating?"

"Come on, you can fess up," 'Viv' said like a dog protecting her property.

"It's okay, Vivian. Those are just jokes."

Vivian looked confused for a moment. She had believed his narrative tooth-and-nail, but now that it was confronted with the angry truth it had changed. She wasn't sure what was correct or what to do with the real Sophie in front of her.

"Wait, so, she didn't—"

Matt quickly interrupted in an attempt to override any

kind of fight with his current girlfriend in front of his ex-girlfriend. "Sophie. Look, it's all for my act. It's comedy. We have to exaggerate the truth a little. You understand."

"No! I don't. It's comedy at my expense. And those things are hurtful to me and my reputation."

"Well, you did break my heart."

"A year ago, Matt! You've moved on."

"Looks like you haven't," Vivian said. What was this? The Real Housewives? Why was she bringing the drama so hard? All she had to do was stand there and be beautiful. Sophie didn't expect her to have this kind of bite on her.

"Vivian, please—" Matt instantly said.

"Vivian, can you not?"

Vivian stood there, surprised that both of them had asked her to be quiet. Sophie had a feeling she wouldn't really stand for that and she secretly relished the idea of Vivian letting Matt have it later on tonight.

"It's good to see you, Sophie," Matt said with as much faux-kindness as he could muster through his horrible beard. "It really is."

"Oh, is it? Really? Is it so good?"

"Good to see you're still as impossible as ever!" They could have left it at that, but Matt couldn't take Sophie's daring stare as she continued to stand there. It was as if her very presence was demanding an apology from him, but he didn't know what to do. He liked making those jokes about her and he sort of liked that she hated it. He just didn't like that he was getting confronted about it. "Okay. Sophie. I don't mean to offend you. I'm just entertaining people. You understand that, right?"

That was when Vivian jumped in like a loyal sidekick.

"Besides, which do you actually care about? That he offended you or your reputation? It sounds like you're jealous that Matt is successful."

Sophie rolled her eyes. Great. So this was a girl who blamed every little thing on jealousy. She probably also thought that Sophie was jealous of her.

"Jesus Christ. Who is this girl, Matt?"

"My name is Vivian," she said proudly like she was a superhero in the cold open of her titular movie this was the part in the movie where the title credits pop up on stage as the two of them were stuck in a freeze frame.

"I know that much, Vivian, but this is kind of an A/B conversation so can you shut the fuck up?"

"Excuse me?!"

"Don't talk to Vivian that way!" Matt shouted, catching the attention of a few people at the party. Up until that moment the party had been a little too loud to grab anyone's attention. Besides, there were a lot of actors there. Actors had very animated, performative conversations. No one was paying attention to their little performance. Matt turned to Vivian shortly after that outburst to chastise her like a child.

"But, Viv, that maybe was too much. You just met her. Please have some tact."

"I'm not the bad guy here!"

"Thank you," Sophie said.

"It's both of you."

"Okay, fuck off, Vivian. And it's good to see you, Matt, because now I know that I can just go tell jokes, too. And they won't offend you. Only your precious reputation."

"Wait, what do you mean—"

Sophie turned around to see Fred watching this encounter only steps away, standing awkwardly by himself in the middle of the room. He was still holding her snack plate. She reached into it and grabbed some more chips to stuff into her mouth. Fred didn't say anything. He just stared at her like he was amazed she said any of that. She was sure that she had either scared him away for good or made him her number one fan.

Tally came up to them with wide eyes that said 'what was that?'

"I gotta go," Sophie said.

"Where?" she asked.

"I'm going to go tell some new jokes right fucking now. I'll go to Simon's show. He'll let me go up."

Tally sighed and walked up, washing her hands clean of the situation. Some new guests came in just then and it was her duty to continue hosting the party. Sophie went into Tally's posh bedroom to grab her coat from a mess of coats on the bed. Fred followed her in and stood beside her as she rummaged for her black coat in the pile of a thousand black coats.

"Can I come?" he asked.

"To the show?"

He leaned in and whispered to her, "I'm really bored here."

Sophie finally found her coat. As she put it on she told him, "I'm about to do something I've never done before."

Fred grabbed a red puffy coat from the pile. He put it on and said, "Yeah, your thing sounds more fun."

"All right, then," she said.

As the two of them walked out the door together, Matt eyed them cautiously. Sophie liked that Matt watched them leave and she hoped he was wondering if they were leaving together. She hoped that he would find out this guy had a cool job. She hoped that that he found out what she was about to do...if it worked, of course.

SEVEN

Fred had been talking the entire bus ride to Lincoln Lodge, the show that Sophie was trying to convince her dear "friend" Simon to let her do a set on. It was one of the absolute best shows in town and had the reputation of being the longest running independent comedy show in the country.

Fred had been talking for a while, but Sophie wasn't paying attention. She was in her head, carefully constructing exactly what she was going to say.

"...You know what I mean? Sophie?"

"Aw, that sucks."

"It sucks that I won a spelling bee?"

"What? Sorry...wait, are you really talking about a spelling bee?"

"No, just wanted to see if you were paying attention."

"No, I'm not paying attention. It's not you, it's me."

"Or maybe it is me. I often worry that I'm a very boring person to be around."

That felt like the beginning of an entirely different conversation and she knew she didn't have the attention to be empathetic to those feelings. She could relate to that. She felt like she wasn't very fun off-stage, but she was focused on her mission right now. She had to let Fred know that.

She pulled the string to get off the bus and as they stood up to exit, she began to tell him, "No, honestly. You're not boring. Or, I mean, I barely know you, so what do I know? So far, I'd say you're pretty entertaining."

He blushed.

"I'm just - okay, quick thing about me: I've been doing comedy for years. I started when I was 19 and no one warned me about adult men. That just doesn't happen. I was 19 and they were all in their mid-twenties. Or older! I got all this attention from these comedians and I loved it, so I dated people. But, like, the way I was used to dating as a teenager. Like 'who cares, this is casual, we're in the same math class'. I didn't think these people would be around forever. But that's how comedy goes. The people you start with are in your class until you die."

"Or quit."

"Which is basically dying."

She remembered the amount of truly funny people she had known along the way who had already given up on comedy. They rarely quit altogether. It was often a slow process of dwindling shows, no new jokes, and a sudden high percentage of bombing at any shows they would be booked at. The joy was sucked out like a steady vacuum until they ultimately started preferring staying at home to hanging out in the back rooms of bars, listening to mediocre jokes until it was their turn to tell them. It happened to so many people she knew. It was like natural selection for comedians.

"I only have one ex-girlfriend and she's many miles away now," Fred said.

That took Sophie out of it for a moment.

"You only have *one* ex-girlfriend?"

"Like, a serious one. We were together for four years until she decided she didn't love me anymore. You know, that old thing."

Sophie felt a tenderness toward Fred stirring from her tummy like she had just drank warm cider. She had been so obsessed with her problems all evening that it felt nice to hear someone else relate their story and not demand any of her help for it.

"That's sweet that you had long term love. I haven't had much success in relationships."

"Every relationship is different."

She knew that and yet hers somehow all seemed the same. They all had patterns and milestones and intense cries followed by intense orgasms. They all had meeting each other's people and magical late night kisses and small fights that snowballed and jealous exes and friends to be suspicious of because they seemed too touchy and fights over *that* and fizzle outs and shoddy breakup attempts and passionate reunions and regrets and blocked numbers. They all felt the same.

"I've only dated comedians. And comedians, while being so very funny and smart, tend to be inconsiderate. And needy. And insecure. And jealous. And, well, just not good."

"Are you including yourself in that?"

"Yeah. I am."

"Ah, so there's your problem. It's bound to explode when both people are like that."

"Correct."

"Why haven't you ever talked about it onstage before? It seems to bother you and you seem so…fearless."

Fearless? He thought she was fearless? That made her feel all fuzzy inside. She often felt like a coward. She was afraid of offending people she knew and she felt like she didn't really talk about anything important on stage. And in real life? She felt like she just sabotaged herself. Fearlessness was something she equated with bravery and bravery belonged to heroes. She never thought of herself as a hero.

"Thanks. I don't think I'm really fearless. You just caught me in a particularly angry moment back there. But usually I don't try to upset people I know or previously dated. I thought that was the right thing to do. You know? Protect these guys or what we had."

Fred nodded. He looked at her from the corner of his eyes affectionately. She felt listened to and admired. This was a new feeling! She could definitely get used to this.

"But I don't want to do the right thing anymore. I'm tired of protecting people. I want to fuck shit up."

They arrived at Lincoln Lodge, where the two of them stood outside the door. Fred opened the door for her and awkwardly said, "Go fuck shit up then!"

She paused before going through the door as if it was symbolic of going through a threshold to a new phase in life. A phase where she would hopefully stop protecting the feelings of people who didn't care about her own feelings. She turned to Fred, whose dark brown eyes were warmly fixed on her.

"Thank you, Fred. Thank you for letting me tell you all that. I know I just met you like forty-five minutes ago, so that's cool of you."

"No, we met five years ago," he said with eyebrows forming into a confused arch.

"What?!"

"Joking!"

Oh, no! She couldn't even tell what a joke was. How was she supposed to go onstage and tell what's funny?!

"Oh, my God, Fred! I can't do this. I don't even know what's funny right now."

He would have none of it. He placed his hand on her back and pushed her through the door, through her imaginary threshold. Fred pushed Sophie into the Lincoln

Lodge, a long-running stand up show that was known for featuring countless great comedians. Sophie had been on the show before, but it was certainly unusual for her to show up like that and ask to go up. Now that she was in the building she was unsure if Simon would actually let her go on. He might be offended by her audacity. Comics who ran good shows were like that. They wanted you to treat them with the respect of a mafioso.

She was on a mission, so she didn't give herself too much time to reconsider. She found that most decisions in her life were best made spontaneously - before she could talk herself out of them. She was already here, so there was no use in backing out.

Simon saw Sophie as he stood by the box office of theater in his signature bow-tie. She hated a comic with a gimmick, but at the same time Simon had a signature look and he was booked more than her. So maybe he knew what he was doing.

"Sophie! You watching the show tonight?"

"I need to go up."

Simon laughed incredulously. Like she was accusing him of a crime. "Just gettin' straight to it, huh?"

"Simon, please? I've got new shit tonight. Like fresh, raw stuff I've never done before."

"But this is a good show - not an open mic."

"It's all about Matt."

Simon's eyes widened as if he had been waiting for her to do Matt material forever. Everyone probably was. Most of the Chicago comedy scene knew he was profiting off jokes about her and they were probably wondering when she was going to swing back.

"Oh, damn. Okay, I'll get you up. Is it okay if it's just six minutes? Not a lot, but—"

"Yeah, anything. I'll even do five. Get me up there."

Simon turned to the eager young male comic next to

him, who was scrutinizing over his jokes in his hand-held notebook. His hands looked huge compared to the tiny notebook that held his big ideas.

"Hey, you have to do less time cause Sophie is going up, too."

The guys looked up, noticing Sophie for the first time. His jaw tightened, but he had never spoken to her before so he didn't want to unleash his fury on her. He leaned into Simon and said in a whisper that was still loud enough for Sophie to hear, "What, is she fucking you?"

"THIS is why I've got to get up there."

"She has new shit, man. What are you gonna do? Tell that boring bus joke again? Sometimes buses go right past you at the bus stop, big deal."

"Hey! It's a good joke! It's relatable!"

Sophie shrugged at the guy.

"I relate to it."

She grinned - which may have been too over the top - and walked with Simon backstage. She watched as he took the stage, always the professional, asking the crowd if they had been to the show before. He asked people if they were from out of town and did some off-the-cuff jokes about their hometowns. These were all host tricks that made the audience comfortable. It was cheesy, but it was necessary. It was the lubrication needed for the bevy of dick jokes that were sure to follow.

"We have a full line-up tonight, ladies and gentlemen. It's gonna be a good night here at the Lincoln Lodge. You ready to get started? I won't even bore you with my hilarious jokes cause that'll waste too much time. I want to kick off the night with my hilarious friend and beautiful lady, Sophie Martin!"

Sophie entered the stage and shook Simon's hand, giving him a smile. He gave her a firm handshake in return as if to say "knock 'em dead". She looked out into the crowd and smiled and waved like she always did. She used to always feel like she was being placed onstage for slaughter, but for the first time she felt like she was about to talk to her friends. That was her mindset. Go out there and talk to this crowd like they are your friends. She wondered why she had never had this approach before.

She looked out into the crowd and didn't recognize anyone immediately. She saw some people standing in the back - comics - looking at her with their arms folded across their chest. She knew what they were thinking: what possessed her to demand to be on the show tonight? The gall of Sophie Martin. Who did she think she was?

Then she saw Fred. Fred smiled from her in the back. He must have seen her looking at him. Or maybe she was looking for him. He was her only genuinely friendly face, so she focused in on him and smiled.

"Hey, folks," she said. Whenever she felt like she might lose them, she decided to look at Fred. Yes, she only just met him, but he had no reason to dislike her. Yet.

"Give it up for our host Simon Heywood, everyone. What a hottie, right? right? I just want to host a show so I can bring up men the way that women are brought up. Our next comedian is a man - can you believe it? Yes, folks, it's 2018 and men CAN be funny! They really do it all."

The crowd tittered. Okay, she was warming them up. They were down.

"Your next comic is a total beefcake, a 7/10, would bang. Let's see if this beefcake is as funny as his flannel shirt warrants!"

More laughs. They were liking it so far. She wasn't killing, but she had their full attention. She loved feeling that. She loved it when she knew they were listening. She was setting up her play, now to spike it.

"It's ridiculous. The more adjectives about my appearance

that I'm brought up to, the more I expect the audience just wants me to sing "Happy Birthday, Mr. President" in my best Marilyn. You know?"

She donned a ditzy Marilyn Monroe impression to coo at the crowd: "'Oh you really are good audience, aren't you? The stage is too hot! I have to take off my clothes. Oops! There goes my virginity.'"

People were really laughing now.

"It's such a double standard. My male comedian friends can fuck whoever they want and they are never slut-shamed. I break up with my boyfriend for not having sex with me and all I hear is that Sophie Martin is a big, fat whore. Like, first of all, when is a size 4 fat? Size 6 on some days, but still. And secondly, that story is true. I dated a guy for about eight months and I was happy! He was really sweet. The guy I saw before him was a tad abusive - just a tad, just a smidge - so I was grateful to date someone who was essentially a 1950's teenager. 'Why, gee, Miss Sophie, I couldn't possibly touch you for fear my penis will turn communist. We should sleep in separate beds to resist temptation and the Red Scare that is your period.'"

Some women in the front row were clapping along with their laughter. That was called clapter. Clapter meant they really agreed with you, more than they thought you were funny. It was never something she was going for. She didn't want to be a comedian who made "points". But then again - maybe she should try it. She was leaning into it and it was working, at least for tonight.

"Seriously! We never had sex. Okay, never is an exaggeration. We had sex like once a month as if a full moon made him turn horny. When I brought it up, he didn't even notice. He was like "we have sex plenty!" As if it's almost too much, you know? Ugh, I hate orgasms! I love a clean, dry pussy. You know?"

She was on fire. It felt like she was racing on a tide and she was taking the lead. All she had to do was spring to the finish line.

"He said - and this is true- 'I like sex just fine, it just doesn't really do it for me. I don't need it.' Which is how I feel about lollipops. Can do without, but if I'm in a dentist's office, sure why not? I like blow-jobs and retainers about the same amount."

She put the microphone back on the stand - the comic's sign that they were about to make their grand conclusion.

"I know this was a little crass, so if you have a problem with this set then...you can eat me out until next Tuesday cause he never did. I'm not gonna not fuck a guy for eight months and not talk about it. You know what I mean?"

She waved at the crowd and grinned from ear-to-ear.

"Thank you, everyone. Goodnight!"

With that she left the stage and heard the excited applause behind her as Simon took the stage again and told everyone to keep it going for her.

She spent most of the show smiling to herself in the back as comics congratulated her. She could always tell when she actually impressed a comic. They would say things like "Really good set" instead of just "good set". They would say things like "seriously, I mean it" after their compliment to indicate that all of their other compliments were just meaningless words. This time? This time it was the real deal.

When the show ended, audience members crowded around her to compliment her. Other comics were asking her for her availability soon to be on their shows. Thank goodness she recorded the set on her phone so she could attempt to recreate the magic. Perhaps it was time to throw away her old goofy observational jokes. These new, edgy jokes might be what actually worked for her. Maybe she would finally get the attention and respect she really wanted as a comic.

She had to make it somehow.

"That was pretty damn cool," Simon said to her as he literally patted her on the back.

"Thanks. It felt good, I think. I don't know yet."

"Come on. You can feel it."

She nodded with a blushing, beaming smile. "I guess so."

"You were in another element. Like you leveled up."

Just then Fred walked up to her. She had sort of forgotten about him after she got off stage, which is crazy because he was her anchor when she got onstage. She wanted to tell him that, but thought he might find it odd.

Fred seemed shy around her suddenly. Maybe he didn't like her jokes. Maybe he felt like he was funnier, more sophisticated. He was a professional humor writer, after all. She suddenly wondered how she really did up there. It was weird considering she didn't know Fred really at all, but she felt overcome with this need for him to like her. Specifically, for him to think she was funny.

"Hey, that was awesome," he said.

"Fred! Oh, my god, thank you so much for coming with me. I mean it—"

"I'm gonna head out, but see you around?"

She felt like she owed him a drink or something. She wanted to hang out with him more and find out what he really thought. But why push it? He said good job and she felt that she should really take a compliment. Few things are less attractive than insisting someone's compliment was wrong.

"Sure," she said like a real cool girl.

Fred's lips curled into a tiny smile and he headed out into the cold alone. Before Sophie could think too much about him, more comics came up to her and invited her out for a drink. She usually fretted about late night hangouts. She always let her anxiety over whether people actually wanted her around get the better of her. But tonight? She felt like she was actually wanted. She had done well, so they all wanted a piece. If show business had taught her anything so far it was that people wanted to be around someone who was actually talented. That was what made Fred leaving so strange.

Sophie came home later than usual - 2 in the morning. That wasn't late for most comics, but it was late for her. She usually became overwhelmed late at night and genuinely felt that you only stayed out past midnight if you were looking to go home with someone that night. She hated feeling like a thirsty vampire prowling a dark bar for a handsome stranger at night, giving him Bela Lugosi eyes to get him alone.

She was surprised to see her roommate Sumi still awake and watching TV in the living room.

"Hey," she said.

"Hey, Sophie," Sumi said back. "I'm kind of high."

Oh. That was why she was - wait, what was she watching?

Sophie sat down on the couch to get a better look at their small, flat screen TV. There he was Matt. In a commercial.

"Isn't that your ex-boyfriend?" Sumi asked.

"Yeah," Sophie said, as if she didn't really know him. As if she didn't actually see him tonight. As if she hadn't done one of her most exciting sets ever based on him. All of that seemed to wash away seeing him on TV. That was the funny thing about seeing someone you knew on TV - they no longer felt like someone you knew. They were now someone everyone knew, someone that was broadcasted into every home in America.

"That's cool he's on TV," Sumi said. "It's like you're famous by association."

"He isn't famous," Sophie scoffed.

"He's on TV."

"Yeah. So? A lot of people are and you don't even know

their name."

"Yeah...but you're not."

Just like that her good night went from a ten to a zero. She went to bed.

EIGHT

Sophie had been on the phone with Tally for several minutes now. First to chew her out for the party and then to thank her because it inspired her. None of this would be a problem if this phone call wasn't interrupting her lunch with Arnie at Pick Me Up Diner. He was grumpily chomping on a BLT across from her as if every bite was a nagging tug on her shoulder to get off the phone.

"I'm telling you, Sophie, people are talking," Tally said. She insisted that she had already heard about her set at Lincoln Lodge, but Sophie wasn't sure if she could trust that. She felt like agents not only said what they thought you wanted to hear, but acted like they had their finger on the pulse of everything. "You gotta keep doing what you did the other night. It's working for you."

"I can't believe word got to you already."

"Word spreads fast when you crush it like that. Do what you did at that dinky little show at the Laugh Factory tomorrow, okay? Who cares about your old jokes about your family? This stuff is working."

"Thanks, Tally. I really have to go."

"I'll be at the show tomorrow. Break legs."

"Thanks, Tally. Bye!"

Sophie put away her phone to see that Arnie was cleaning his plate with his french fries.

"You already finished your lunch?"

"Would it kill you to tell Tally to take me on as a client?"

"I have before!" She didn't want Arnie to think she wouldn't help him out, because she definitely would, but so much of this business was out of her hands. All she could do was recommend him. It was up to Tally to take him on as a client.

"Maybe she'll listen now that you're making waves."

"The Laugh Factory. I've never been able to get onstage there beyond a mic."

"Proud of you, kid."

"But, like...how do I capture lightning twice?"

"This is your new voice! You've got to try it on for a while to see if it sticks."

The door opened and Sophie could see a familiar long face with oval glasses poking around the diner, looking for a seat. It was Fred. He was wearing an interesting salmon-colored coat that looked like it was lifted from someone's dad in the seventies. He saw her and smiled. She waved him over.

"Who are you waving at?" Arnie asked.

"It's Fred."

"Who?"

Arnie turned over his shoulder to see him. He smirked. "You picked up another fanboy the other night?"

Fred came to the table grinning. Looked like he wasn't disgusted by her comedy after all. Or perhaps he was just really polite.

"Hey, Sophie! Hi, I'm—"

"Fred?" Arnie said, staring at Fred's outstretched hand that was inviting a shake.

"Mindreader?" He asked, withdrawing the hand.

She hated that comics did this sometimes. Sometimes they were really rude to people they deemed to be regular. It was as if they thought acting like an asshole gave them a special mystique.

"I'm Arnie Palermo."

"Do I have to call you by both names?"

"Stop the witty reporte, you two! I feel like I'm seated at the Algonquin Roundtable."

Fred laughed. His face was really cute when he laughed. He had one dimple on his left side that made most of his smiles seem smirk-like.

Arnie didn't get the reference. He stared between the two of them, but Sophie couldn't tell what he was thinking. He was probably crabby that his lunch had been interrupted twice.

"Oh, it's a reference I don't get. You're a freaking nerd, Sophie."

"Nerd wasn't working for me, though. Angry, tell-all ex-girlfriend is my new thing!"

"I kind of like that thing," Fred said.

Hey - he liked it! Kind of. She tried not to read into it. Arnie got his stuff together suddenly and threw a couple dollar bills onto the table. Sophie hoped he wasn't short-changing her out of spite.

"Nice to meet you, Fred. But I'm done with my food."

"What? You're leaving?"

"You were talkin'! I finished! You still have food and Fred is here. So...Adios."

Arnie gave a fake little bow and slipped his pea-coat on. He looked over his shoulder as he was leaving to raise his eyebrows at Sophie. Sophie rolled her eyes at him. All the while Fred was standing there, unsure of what to do. Did she have to invite him to sit down like a ghoul that can't enter a house without being invited?

"Um…shall I or are you waiting on Robert Benchley?"

She blushed. She couldn't help it. He really was smart. She was a lifelong and avid comedy nerd, but not a lot of comics she met were. They could rattle of Bill Burr jokes, but they didn't know any history. They didn't know about humorists and vaudeville, radio shows and cabarets. Arnie did love a lot of it, but she had such an encyclopedic knowledge that she often found herself making annoying references alone.

She quietly gestured for Fred to sit.

"What are you doing here? You live near here?"

"Not really. I'm in Pilsen," he said. Sophie couldn't help but make a face. Pilsen was so far from this little diner in Wrigleyville, a neighborhood that was even far for Sophie. Arnie insisted on it, however. It was his favorite place and it was close to the coffee shop he worked at. Arnie was a sweet friend who was always insisting on his own conveniences above all others.

"That's a long way from Kansas, Toto."

"Well, I figured I wasn't in Kansas anymore." He bit his lip. Was he nervous about joking around with her? She just figured he must have thought he was better than her. "I was running an errand and wanted to get something to eat. It's unbelievable how much of the city I've never seen."

"Really?"

"Yeah! I wonder if I'll ever feel "at home" in Chicago."

"Do you miss New York?"

"I do. I miss the people. I feel like you just miss any place that has the people you love, though."

"But do you like being in Chicago?"

Fred laughed to himself. In certain lights he looked like a hot professor with those round glasses. In other lights he just looked like a normal humor writer in a baggy sweater. What was with his baggy sweaters?

"Chicagoans always need to know if you like it."

And she did. She wanted to know. She needed to know. She needed that validation.

"Well? Do you?"

"I do! But I wish I knew it better. I feel like a tourist with no tour guide."

Sophie looked down at her half-eaten chicken wrap. She was done with it. Fred had distracted her from having an appetite.

"What are you doing today?"

"I was just gonna write. Not much for a Saturday."

Sophie leaned in like she had a dirty secret. Her head got low and Fred followed suit, leaning in to meet her like they were about to discuss top secret plans.

"I see," she said. "Because I was going to do that, too - write - but I also love showing off my city."

"Go on."

"You're talkin' to the city's number one tour guide for writing hot spots."

Fred and Sophie left Pick Me Up and walked up Clark Street a short way to Wrigley Field. Sophie wasn't a baseball fan, but it was hard not to admire the legacy of the Cubs. She lived in Chicago when they actually broke the curse and won the World Series. It was so exciting that even she got in the spirit.

They stood outside of Wrigley Field and looked up at the pic, historic sign.

"Baseball fan?"

"Is that the one on ice?"

"No, that's the other one."

"I do love figure skating."

She smirked. Cool, so he wouldn't make her watch baseball. If they were dating. God, why did her brain go there? They were just hanging out. They hadn't even kissed.

He could have a weird dick. *Chill out, psycho.*

"We could take a selfie. You know - to blend into the environment?"

They looked around. That was all anyone around them was doing. It was a cold Saturday in Chicago and people were still huddled together in front of Wrigley Field for a picture. They stood close together, trying to get in the frame of Fred's phone. He smelled good like rose and wood. Like incense.

A Cubs fan was walking by and shouted at full volume: "GO CUBS!!!"

Really, sir? It's one in the afternoon. Lower your voice.

"Is this really an ideal writing spot?" Fred asked.

"No, I just thought I'd be a good tour guide. Come on."

She was coming up with a plan in her head of places to take him and she was super excited about it.

He followed her onto the Clark Street bus, where they sat close together and talked about the city. Fred talked about the restaurants in Pilsen that he liked. Their knees were kind of close together. At one point they touched and neither of them pulled away. Fred instead just talked about how he couldn't think of good Mexican restaurants in Montreal.

"Or New York, really," he added. "They probably exist, but I didn't eat at them. It's all I eat now."

"Oh! Wait, stop talking," Sophie said. She pointed out the window. "I think it's right about here. Here is where the Valentine's Day Massacre happened."

"What is that?" Fred asked.

"You never heard of it?" she asked. She reached over him to pull the lever on the bus. They stood up to get off the bus.

"It's this unsolved mob hit from the 20's," she explained. She became cautious of people overhearing her talk. What if some mob dude was on the bus? Or a super squeamish person? "That used to be a garage and all these people were gunned down in it. Mob guys. They thought it was Capone, but no one could ever pin it on him."

"How romantic," he said.

"What?"

"Valentine's Day. What a way to say I love you."

They walked out into the cold in the heart of Lincoln Park.

"You're kind of morbid, you know that?" she said.

"You're the one loudly pointing out historic crime scenes."

They walked in the cold over to Oz Park, a gem of a park that Sophie loved. She could still remember the first time she came there. It was at night, so she thought it was way bigger than it actually was. She also thought it was magical - this park with statues from the Wizard of Oz. What a dreamy place!

It was pretty cold, below thirty for sure, which was actually kind of warm for a Chicago January. She began to wonder if Fred was resenting this journey.

"Behold. Oz Park: home of Chicago's only statue of a woman in park."

They looked up to see a statue of Dorothy with Toto at her feet.

"Who is it?"

"Dorothy. From the Wizard of Oz."

Fred stared at the statue with a furrowed brow. That's the response she had hoped for. "Wait…so a fictional woman?"

"Oh, you thought women were real?" she joked.

"Wow," he said thoughtfully. "So this is really the only park in the whole city that has a female statue?"

"Yep. Some of the colleges have statues of women in history, but even those you can count on one hand."

"Looks like I'm really not in Kansas anymore."

She smiled at him.

"Are you cold?"

"Take me to a warm writing spot."

"Well, I have another idea"

They walked south a few blocks on Lincoln Avenue to Lincoln Hotel, which sat on Lincoln and Wells Street. Inside the hotel was a cozy coffee shop open to the public. She had heard the hotel had a rooftop with amazing views that was open to the public, but she was too scared to try it. She always feared being kicked out for seeming like riff raff.

Fred was looking all around him, having never been in this very nice part of the city before. The expansive Lincoln Park - the park itself - was across the street and it stood in the way of the beach. Fred hadn't actually seen Lake Michigan yet.

At the cafe Sophie treated the two of them to hot chocolates, but they didn't take their time getting warm. She had places to show him. The next place in mind: Second City.

They walked down Wells Street to the infamous Second City, a building that boasted countless famous alums. Sophie had taken improv classes there, but she had always been more of a stand up comedian. Second City wasn't a place for stand ups, but she still respected the hell out of it.

They sat on the front steps.

"If it were warmer," she said. "We could definitely sit out here and write, but alas."

"If we sit here long enough, will we be as funny as Belushi?"

"We'll be as funny as two Belushis."

Fred arched his back and looked up as if heaven was directly above them.

"Let the power John and Jim wash over me."

They laughed together, neither one trying to impress the other with a quip. The day had felt a little like that, with the two of them volleying little jokes to test one another. Sitting on the steps of a comedy institution, they both felt calmer. They felt in sync.

"Where to next?" Fred asked.

"You sure you aren't too cold?" Sophie asked.

Fred shook his head. He looked genuinely excited to be there. There was a glow in his eyes. He was glowing at her.

"Well...it might get colder."

They walked down North Avenue, but all the way down. Through the beginning of Lincoln Park, next to the history museum, and through statues of prominent men in history. They did this twenty-minute walk to the beach.

The beach was frozen over, which was its own kind of beautiful. There was snow instead of sand and the lake was rippling with chunks of ice.

They stood, looking out into the expansive water. It seemed impossibly big. This lake definitely looked more like an ocean. It was easy to stand at the shore of Lake Michigan and feel like you were standing at the edge of the world.

"Wow," Fred said. "It's easy to forget that this is a city with a beach."

Sophie breathed in the crisp air. It was certainly colder by the lake. The air was so frigid it was starting to freeze her nose hairs, but she didn't mind it for once. She loved standing next to Fred on the shore where no one else was. It was the two of them at the end of the Earth.

"I love it." She looked over at him and watched him gaze out into the distance. Maybe he was trying to see Michigan. "What's it like to live close to the ocean?"

"I've never lived close to the ocean—"

"In New York! You lived closer to the ocean than I ever have."

"Oh. I never thought of it like that."

"I would. I would be bowled over by it."

She looked out again. She wondered who the first people to explore the lake were. History taught about explorers sailing out to prove the Earth was round and hitting land. Who were the first people to venture out into the lake and find themselves hitting another piece of land?

"Whenever I would go to Coney Island and stand on the shore, I would look out and remember the rest of the world is out there." He looked at her again. "Which is kind of how I feel right now."

"Except it's Michigan that's out there. And Gary, Indiana."

"Honestly? It looks the same. It's just as incredible."

There was no sarcasm, no juicy joke, no tension or turn. They weren't joking at all. They were being open with each other. For the first time all day she felt like she could turn off. There was no need to be funny or snarky. She could just be.

"That's really sweet."

It hit Sophie that she still barely knew Fred. She had met him less than twenty-four hours ago and was spending all day with him. Was this normal? Didn't he want to go home?

"Okay, tour guide. Show me more."

"There's only one more place I have in mind."

Sophie wasn't sure if the final stop on her tour would be impressive. In fact, she knew it was underwhelming. But she felt compelled to show it to him. It was her favorite spot in the city. Her quiet spot. A spot that likely only meant anything to her because she stumbled upon it during one sunny August afternoon and it felt magical to her. It was one of those places that made her grateful to live in the city she lived in.

Fred and Sophie sat quietly on a bench in front of the Midwest Buddhist Temple. It seemed so out of place for the neighborhood, which felt like a small European gem in the middle of this huge Midwestern city. The streets in this corridor in Old Town were brick and narrow with long, old houses that felt like they belonged on the East Coast, lining the streets like a village in the 1800's. There, in the middle of all that quaintness, stood a large Japanese temple. It was sleek in design, as if it had been built in the 50's or 60's at the height of modernism, but it was still distinctly Japanese. The temple sat at a dead-end street and a lovely little park was right in front of it. The park was small and only full of benches, a chess table, and a fountain. It was lovely and it felt like hers.

"This is my favorite spot in the whole city."

Fred looked around, noting that no one was near them.

"This feels so tucked away," he said. "Like it's not supposed to be here."

"I know." She smiled. His brown eyes sparkled back at her. She noticed flecks of gold in them.

"How did you even find out about this?"

"I was taking a class at Second City. Improv."

"Oh? The most respected art form."

"Hey, it was fun!" She laughed as she let her memory stroll down into the rose-colored recesses of her mind to replay the footage of her walking around that August day. "I used to walk around the neighborhood before class because I was so nervous. Every class, I was terrified. Like I was thinking I'd somehow be discovered in class or like it meant something big. I was like 19, so this was my first step into comedy. Naturally, I had no idea how anything worked."

"Sure, how could you?" Fred said. "I still don't."

She ignored him because, in her mind, he did. He had a real comedy writing job. She was still working part-time in retail.

"This neighborhood is so beautiful and full of history, so I felt a lot of peace walking around. I always liked picturing comedians doing the same, like Tina Fey or Rachel Dratch or someone. Anyway, one day I come across this temple and there is this huge festival going on for this Japanese holiday called Ginza. It was alive. Like it's quiet right now, but I'm telling you. This place was packed with so much food, dancing, lanterns!"

"Love lanterns."

"I know! So I told my class about it and afterwards we all came over here and it was gone. Like it vanished."

"Whoa. Japanese Brigadoon."

Yes, exactly! That's how it felt!

"Right! So we are left with this quiet, little park."

Fred was smiling at her as she looked out ahead of them. She could feel his eyes on her. She wondered if his eyes were glued to her lips. She felt overcome with the desire to kiss him somehow, but she wasn't sure how to initiate it. Wasn't that funny? She was almost thirty and still felt unsure of first kisses. They never did get easier.

"So I started coming here to think."

She shyly looked at him - shyly now because she was worried her thoughts might be broadcasted out loud. Maybe he would know she wanted to kiss him. Maybe she would know the warmth bubbling inside of her and that it was all for him. She felt nervous and calm and both were because she had spent all day with him. It felt like something big should happen next, but she wasn't sure what.

And then. There. He looked at her lips. He looked at her lips for a moment. It was all she needed to know that he was feeling that, too.

"Thanks for showing me all of this," he said, and then his eyes glanced up to meet hers again. "Really. Today was so cool."

"There's just something about you. I feel like I'm constantly spilling my heart out. I don't really know you. You could be a psycho."

He shrugged playfully. "I guess I could be a psycho. I don't know that about myself either, so we can both find out together."

"Oh, cool! That's just what a psycho would say."

They laughed. She could feel it getting colder out which meant it must be late in the day. That's when she realized that she had no idea what time it was. The entire afternoon had gotten away from her and now the sky was breaking into streams or orange and purple light. She pulled out her phone to check the time, a single action that seemed to break the magic of the moment.

It was 4:30 in the evening. Early, but late for winter. The darkness was coming soon.

"I should really get going."

She stood up, waiting for him to stand too.

"What, um, what are you doing tonight? Like a show or—"

Sophie shook her head. She sat back down.

"Oh it must be big if you had to sit down for this."

They were watching each other's lips again. She could feel their thighs touching. Being close to him felt necessary to combat the cold. She told herself it was simply necessary.

"No. Actually, I don't have anything. Maybe I'll watch a show or just see a movie and be at home for once—"

They were so close to each other.

"We're - um - really close to each other right now."

They looked at each other's lips again. His seemed oh so kissable, but it felt like too much. What were they going to do? Make out in the cold and get snot all over each other? How sexy would that be? She looked away. She had an idea.

"Want to come over for dinner?"

Fred seemed surprised. Maybe he wasn't thinking all of the things she was thinking, but how could that be possible?

Surely she wasn't living in a vacuum on that bench.

"Can you cook?" he asked.

"Can I cook! Ha! Let's find out."

NINE

Fred and Sophie were hanging out in Sophie's kitchen. Sumi was out for the night, so they were blasting music from Sophie's phone - using the speakers Sumi left in the kitchen - as they split a box of pizza and wine. The upbeat song ended and the next thing that played was...a comedy track.

"Oh my God!" Sophie said in a panic, scared for a minute that it might be a recording of herself at an open mic. "Sorry! I just put it on shuffle."

"Is that you?"

"No! I'm not Kanye West."

"You think Kanye makes out to his own music?"

Sophie looked at Fred as if to say "duh" and pressed forward to the next song. Once it kicked in she felt the song throughout her whole body. *Yessssss.*

"This. Is. My. Favorite. Song."

It took Fred a few seconds to identify it, or maybe he was distracted by Sophie's swaying to the sensual slow beats of Prince's "The Beautiful Ones".

"This is Prince, right?"

"Who else?" she asked.

"This is really your favorite song?"

"Of course! I love Prince."

"Wow. I don't know too many genuine Prince fans."

Sophie pointed to herself with her wine glass as she continued to bob around sexily to the music. She was up on her feet ready to pour herself more wine as Fred sat at the kitchen table and drunk her in.

"I'm one of them, baby."

She wasn't sure if it was the wine or the song or the look in Fred's eyes as he watched her or her tight jeans, but she felt really fucking sexy all the sudden. It was just the two of them, in her apartment alone, and they were listening to her favorite song. She felt in control and control made her feel powerful. Power was sexy.

"Did you ever see him live?"

"YES! I did, actually."

Sophie placed her glass on the table and picked up Fred's for a re-fill. They were all in for getting good and wine-drunk together which was a fuzzy kind of reddish drunk that felt heavy and playful.

"It was incredible," she said as she took a seat at the table. They raised their glasses to each other again - for about the third time tonight - as she recounted seeing her favorite musician. "It had to have been 2012 maybe. 2013? He packed the United Center and he made us wait in the dark for an hour for an encore."

She hummed along to the song for a moment, feeling absolutely no self-consciousness about breaking into song at any time.

"Wait, what? You all thought there might be an encore, so you stayed?"

"Yes! It's Prince!"

"But why did you all wait around?"

She looked at him like, 'Are you serious?' Like, it was a crime to not wait around. It was Prince. A living icon. Who wouldn't wait?!

"Because we knew it was coming! I swear to God he had a stagehand come out with a flashlight and a dustpan to clean up the stage and the lights were out the whole time. The guy was cleaning the stage with a tiny handheld flashlight."

"That sounds abusive."

"Okay, true. But when he finally came out and it was so worth it. It was Prince! In his element! Dancing in those heels nonstop. Shredding on his guitar. Amazing."

"I admire your dedication."

She became very aware that she had been talking for a while, but nothing in its body language - or actual language - indicated that he wanted her to stop. He seemed to be baiting her, as if fishing for the perfect line. The line for what? She smiled seductively at him as she stood up again.

"You gotta wait for something you know is worth it, right?"

"Right," he said and looked at her like she had just recited poetry. She could feel it in that moment that she was desirable. Or at least that he was desiring her and no matter how old she got or how many experiences like this she had had - it always felt good to be wanted.

"So you love a spectacle?" he asked with a raised eyebrow as he watched her get a glass to fill with water. Perhaps they had had too much wine in too little time.

"No. I love a performance. On stage. I don't like real life spectacles."

"No grand gestures."

"Definitely not. No prom-posals—"

"I'll make a note of that when ask you to prom."

"—or princess weddings."

"I thought all little girls dreamed of those things."

"I'm not like other girls!" Sophie said in a fakey voice to let Fred know that she was aware that was a dumb thing to believe. More than anything, she just wanted to listen to the music. She threw back her head and let the music weave in and out of her thoughts. This song was simply too beautiful to be background music. "But then again, I've always loved to perform. I'm not trying to be like one of those 'I'm not like other girls' girls. I just don't like the performance of it all. I think those things - they're little performances in and of themselves, you know? They demand attention and ask other people to look at your private life."

"But you talk about your private life on stage."

"Yes! But I control it. You know? And it's heightened."

"Yeah, it's you, but it's a persona."

"Exactly! It's not 100% real. The real stuff? Like true love, big apologies, and important moments...I want those to be meaningful. I want them to be real."

Sophie started singing along quietly, and Fred watched her. It was ramping up to her favorite part - when Prince got very emotional as he declared his love for this beautiful woman.

"*What's it gonna be, baby?*" Prince asked through the speakers.

"Oh, wait, I love this part." She made eyes with Fred and sang to him, doing a kind of Prince impression with her gyrating hips and fake pout.

"Do you want him? Or Do you want me? Cause I want you!"

Sophie pointed emphatically at Fred and said again, "Cause I want you!"

He laughed, feeling a little awkward about her sudden performance right after she decried public performances of affection. There she was, in her kitchen, performing for an audience of one. She grabbed a spatula from her sink - it was unclear if it was dirty or clean - and sang into it like a mic.

"Listen to me. I may not know where I'm goin' babe."

Fred watched her with laser focus. His smile went away and it was replaced by a hungry look.

"I said I may not know what I need."

He stood up, eyes focused on hers like a tiger hunting down prey. He was walking toward her as she fake-sang her heart out.

"One thing, one thing's for certain baby. I know what I want, yeah. And if it please you baby..."

She stopped. Her eyes met his as he was standing in front of her now. She backed up to the edge of her kitchen counter and parted her lips. It was her sign that she wanted this. He put his hands delicately on her hips as if the two of them might turn into dust at any moment.

"I want you!"

And then they burst into kissing. She couldn't even identify who did what first or at what volume their passion was turned to, but it felt immediate and strong. Like an explosion.

"I want you! Yes, I do."

The two of them made out in the kitchen until the song ended and they were drawn to her bedroom, where they finished off their seduction with a classic mating ritual.

(Sex. They had sex.)

The two of them laid in her bed, cuddling by the light of her bedside lamp. They were sitting quietly in that after sex stupor that is full of both surprise and warmth. The build-up was gone now that intimacy had been had, but there lingered a tiny whisper of 'what now?' An 80's song that neither of them were particularly listening to was playing as they laid there with arms and legs wound around each other under her fleece blanket to stay warm from the winter chill. They refused to put their clothes back on quite yet. Why ruin the moment with added warmth? She was afraid that once either of them unwrapped from this embrace that it would all fade away. The whole day would officially vanquish into memory.

Suddenly "Whip My Hair" by Willow Smith came on. Sophie was mortified. This was why she played records. How the hell was this on her phone?

"Ugh! The shuffle!" she screeched. She got up, removing her arms from his long body that was much smaller than it appeared under those baggy sweaters he was always wearing. He looked like a string bean. Not in a bad way, it was just what he looked like without the layers of wool.

Fred reached after her as she slipped her panties back on and found her phone to turn off the music.

"No, leave it. I like it," he said.

She shook her head as she clasped her bra back on. "Oh, you like this?"

"The song and the girl in front of me, yeah."

She pretended to lip sync to the mindless Willow Smith song.

"God, I forgot this song existed," Fred said. "Takes me back to high school."

"High school?" Sophie asked, trying to remember when this song was released. "Isn't this only like six old?"

"Maybe eight," Fred said.

"Still!"

"I graduated high school in 2012."

She stopped. Her face fell. What?

"High school?"

"Yeah, when did—"

Oh my god. Was she a predator? How old was he? She was already out of college by then. What the fuck had she just done? She turned off the music abruptly and reached for more articles of clothing. She felt the sudden urge to wrap this whole thing up.

"Oh my god. You're a baby."

"Come on."

"I graduated college in 2012."

"So you're 27?"

"29. A lot closer to 30 than you."

"It's really not that big of an age difference. I'm 23."

"Fucking hell."

"We're adults!"

"Barely."

"I turn 24 in two months."

"I turned 24 five years ago."

"Hey. Come here." She looked at Fred. He was so cute, but it was becoming hard to take him seriously. She kept picturing herself graduating college with him entering high school. Or whatever. She was scared to do the real math in her head.

"It's really not that big of a difference."

"It's kind of freaking me out."

"When you're an adult it doesn't really matter."

Maybe he was right. She didn't think he was young before and he seemed so capable with his real job and career trajectory. Besides, men did these things all the time. Most of the male comics she knew were constantly hitting on 22 year olds and no one batted an eye. It's just that people in their early twenties rarely knew what they wanted. Men liked that. They loved babying their girlfriends and teaching them things. But men didn't seem to want a woman to teach them things. They didn't want replicas of their moms and teachers.

Sophie had been so hopeful and now...it felt like this fun thing had a definite cutoff. It was no longer full of possibility. It felt full of the certainty of him leaving her.

God, why was she already jumping ahead? She wished she could just be chill and live in the moment. She wished she could just hook up without a consequence.

"But you're a young adult," she said as she slipped back

into the bed and into her spot under his arm. It did feel good.

"The young adult section is for thirteen year olds."

"When you were thirteen I was graduating high school."

"Hey. Stop. I'm having fun. Are you having fun?"

She nodded. She was, up until she knew he was significantly younger than her. "Yes."

"Cool. so let's just have fun, yeah?"

They kissed. Now she was back to having fun.

"One thing," he whispered close to her face. "Can I call you Mommy?"

She groaned and pushed him away, but he started tickling her. The trick to get anyone to laugh! They collapsed back into each other until they dozed into dreamland.

TEN

Of course that night with Fred wasn't simply a hookup. Neither of them were really that type of person - especially after spending that entire day together. It felt special, as if they should continue to hang out. So that's what they did. They had hung out together every day for two weeks.

She was even able to have fun at her part-time job - which she really only went to about three or four days a week. She had been working at Bad Girls Vintage for a few years, so she got away with having a lax schedule. Or calling her boss last minute and asking for the afternoon off for an audition, only to hear her tell her that it was very unprofessional for her to keep doing that. But Sophie was never fired. Even when she was convinced she would be fired, she would come in and act like she didn't do anything to piss off her boss. And it worked.

Work was more fun that week because all the oversized 90s sweaters reminded Sophie of Fred. She started setting some aside to gift him. Maybe he'd like this grungy waffle print? Or a denim long-sleeve "sweater" with a corduroy collar? Maybe he would just like anything she gave him because they were in that stage of their infatuation where everything she did was adorable and heavy with meaning.

They usually played throwback hits in the shop, but there was a new girl at work who was very young. So young that she thought it was cute to listen to the radio. She thought that the radio itself was vintage.

"It fits the aesthetic," the eighteen-year-old SAIC art student said.

Sophie was in too good a mood all week to argue, but it was strange when a folk-pop song came on the radio. It had a unique folk-in-the-sixties sound to it with a distinctly modern male voice that sounded both poppy and emotional. Who was this? Mumford and Sons unplugged? New Bright Eyes if Conor Oberst got punched in the gut?

When you call me I come runnin'

From Buffalo to Brooklyn

California skies meet Midwest thighs

I lost you somewhere in between

This voice did sound familiar. So did the somewhat stereotypical and vaguely sexual lyric. Had she heard this song before?

"Who is this?" Sophie asked her younger co-worker that she wasn't ready to admit might be hipper than her. "Is this a new song?"

She shrugged. "Yeah. I heard this the other day, but they didn't say who it was. Kind of cool, right? The guy sounds like he is full of heartache. I love that kind of stuff."

"Like sad songs?"

"Yeah, or like anything where I can tell this man was, like, destroyed. You know? Like I can feel that his life sucks and that's, like, cool. It's hot."

Sophie nodded.

So happy birthday, darlin'. I hope you get your wish—

Wait. No. Was it?

Happy birthday, darlin'. Wish I could be your gift—

"I think I know who this is," Sophie thought out loud.

Her co-worker didn't bother to lift her head from the computer. The DJ's voice came on the radio and said, "That was "Happy Birthday" by the Jose Florian Band."

"Oh, my God," Sophie whispered out loud.

"Is that who you thought it was?"

She nodded. "Yeah. I know him."

"Cool."

It weirdly didn't bother her. Was that song about her? Probably. But perhaps not entirely. She had learned a lesson in applying truth to art and that lesson was that not everything had to be entirely true. Not everything was that raw. It had been five years; surely the subject of that song was an amalgamation of different Sophies that Jose had known throughout the years. It was an ode to all the bitches who broke his heart and their miserable birthdays.

Rather than feel the pit in her stomach she felt when she heard Matt's jokes aimed at her, she got her target aside. She instead let the song wash over her as she sorted through her pile of sweaters. There was a bright wool and acrylic sweater of different vertical bars that would make him look like the side of an ice cream truck. There was a faded grey sweater with one teal horizontal stripe stretched across the chest and sleeves. Ah, that was such a look back then; the just-missing-the-shoulder stripe look. He probably wouldn't even remember that. He wasn't really around for it.

Sophie truly didn't think about the age difference...unless Fred was talking about high school or college or pop culture, or anything, really. She did keep thinking about it. She kept thinking all it took was one hot twenty-two-year old to catch his attention away from her.

Then she saw it. Sophie saw an olive green, loose knit sweater. This was the one to give Fred. It was warm and the olive would bring out the flecks of gold in his eyes. She wanted to see him wear it and then see him take it right off.

But until then? He would watch her crush with her new jokes at Cafe Mustache.

"I like blow-jobs and retainers about the same amount."

She put the mic back in the mic stand to cue up her new closer. She looked out into the crowd and it was surprisingly packed for an early February show when it was only fifteen degrees outside. But that was Chicago. People had to be used to the cold and brave it if they had any hope of socializing for three-to-five months.

"I'm terrified he might be in the crowd when I'm telling these very true jokes about him, but I'm not going to not have sex with someone for eight months and not talk about it. I mean, guys, I'm a narcissist. This is what I do! Come on! Okay, thank you all, you've been an amazing crowd." She gestured for Arnie to return to the stage. "Let's keep it going for your host, Arnie Palermo."

Arnie returned to the stage as the crowd clapped and cheered. "Sophie Martin, everyone! Let her hear it! And we'll be here next week, folks. Thanks for coming out and thanks to all our amazing comics tonight. Have a goodnight!"

Sophie was feeling increasingly good. These jokes were truly going well and lately she had Fred waiting for her off-stage. He was always grinning at her and never afraid to kiss her as soon as she left stage. She could get used to that. Matt always hated PDA and she and Matt became resentful of one another doing well. One would get off stage to applause and the other would be standing there, arms folded, chewing the bottom look and seeming generally aloof. It was cooler to act like they didn't care than to be proud of one another and they so desperately wanted to seem cool to other comics - and to each other. Showing love, admitting love, being proud of each other - those things were not cool.

Fred, so far, didn't seem to care about cool. He was

wearing an oversized Wyoming sweatshirt. It just said Wyoming on it. His oval glasses and shaggy hair seemed old, but he didn't care. He didn't even seem aware. And that made him extremely cool.

So did the fact that he kissed her in front of her friends.

"Okay, so this is going to for sure be a thing?" Arnie asked, breaking up their fifth post-set kiss.

"Shut up, Arnie," Sophie said.

Simon approached them wearing a polka-dot bow-tie. He wasn't even on the show tonight, but he was dressed like he would be ready to tell jokes at a moment's notice. "Hey, guys! Karaoke? What do you all say?"

"Only if you do a duet with me, Simon," Arnie said. "I'm Cher and you're Sonny."

"Baby, you know I'm always Cher."

"Then I'm out!" Arnie declared. "The gay man gets to be Cher. Them's the rules."

"Let's go," Fred said to Sophie. "I hear Sophie loves karaoke. Right, Sophie?"

They all laughed. Sophie notoriously sat there during karaoke, never picking a song. She claimed she couldn't remember the words to any of the songs and that it was embarrassing to go up there not actually know the words. Everyone knew she was making excuses for not wanting to look stupid.

"Get her some wine and she'll sing Prince," Fred said.

Arnie gave them a look like 'that's too much information'.

"Oh, my god. Get a room, you guys," Arnie said.

"A karaoke room!" Simon shouted. "Come on, everyone! Finish your drinks. Or give me your drink tickets. I'm thirsty and I wasn't on the show -"

Simon stopped talking. He looked up and nudged Sophie. Fuck. It was Matt. And he looked miles from pleased.

"Uh, Sophie—"

"Oh, God. Hi, Matt."

"So nice of you to do those jokes in front of me."

Sophie shrugged. It was the best she could come up with in his face.

"How do you like my new material?"

Matt pinched his lips together as if he was trying to make them disappear. That was his signature move to let others know he was trying to stop himself from exploding. Sophie thought he did it to look intimidating to others, but he was already such a physically hulking figure that he didn't need much to intimidate.

"Can I speak to you privately for a moment?"

Sophie looked around to her friends who were all staring between them wide-eyed. No one wanted to stand up to the semi-famous Matt Kistler. She thought of Fred, who didn't know who he was other than the brief introduction at the party. She remembered he was only 23 and so skinny underneath his clothes. He couldn't take Matt if he had to. She'd have to step in with a roundhouse kick or something she learned from three months of self-defense classes in college.

"No," she said bravely. "You've had no problem airing your grievances against me in public for months now. Why should I give you any kind of privacy—"

"PLEASE." It was loud, but through gritted teeth. He wasn't asking. He was demanding.

"Hey, keep your voice down, Matt," Arnie finally said.

"Get the fuck out of here, Arnie."

"We're all pals here," Simon said, stepping in for some reason. "No need to be hostile—"

"Hey, Simon. Don't you have a burlesque show to host?"

"Ok. Ouch," Simon said as he adjusted his patterned bow-tie.

Matt was a jerk. A huge jerk. He always was one, but it used to be more private. He used to try and be cute about it, posing his insults as party quips. Throwing someone under the bus for the good of others. So everyone would laugh and it would raise Matt above everyone. He always had his victims, the people he would playfully punch on the arm after having thrown them overboard. He'd always say, "Hey, sorry about that. But we were all having fun. Right?"

Now that he was more successful than all of them he was being more open about it. He was insulting her friends - their friends - without recourse.

"Fine," Sophie sighed. "If you're going to be such a baby about this, then I'll give you two minutes. Outside."

Matt followed Sophie outside, steaming behind her. Hey, she could steam, too. He knew that about her. She would always meet his level of anger. That was why they were so toxic for each other. They knew exactly which buttons to press and how hard to press them.

It was instantly brisk outside. Way too cold to have any kind of conversation. She broke the ice by saying, "God, it's so cold out here—"

Matt interrupted her to ask: "What the hell was that?" Straight to the point.

"What?"

"All that me not having sex stuff. That's really, really personal. And honestly? I didn't know it was that big of an issue."

"Oh, my God, Matt. You didn't? Really?"

It was something they definitely talked about - a lot. It made her feel bad and then it made him feel bad. She would feel like a whore for wanting to have sex with her boyfriend more than he wanted to and then she also felt bad about herself. She was insecure that he wasn't attracted to her. All of this, of course, made him feel like something about wrong with him. He never thought that amount they had sex was an issue until she brought it up. These were private circular conversations they would have again and again until they finally broke up. It was private. Sophie had never wanted to embarrass him with jokes about it before. No guy wants someone emasculating them by claiming they didn't fuck. Guys were supposed to fuck. Comics especially. They were supposed to be swimming in women - it was the image they worked so hard to put forth. Sophie doing this onstage was more than just her airing grievances about their relationship. She was exposing him and pointing and laughing while she did it.

"That's not even the point. Now not only do I know it - but everyone we work with knows it. The whole comedy scene is talking about it."

She was starting to feel bad until she reminded herself of his jokes that painted her as a monster. According to him, she was a succubus. Not even a human woman.

"Do I really need to remind you that you told everyone I cheated on you when I didn't?"

"Well, that was way easier to tell everyone than the truth."

"So you know the truth, then."

"It makes me look bad, Soph."

She shook her head and looked away from him. He was pathetic. Despite the success, he was still this insecure. "You always have to be the victim," she muttered.

"Who cares?" he said. "It's comedy and it's just my jokes. No one knows the truth."

"Exactly. Your word against mine. So here's *my* word."

"God, you just can't take the high road, can you?"

The high road? So she was expected to drop this and let him go on stage and say what he wanted. Did he not hear himself?

"I'm sorry, Matt. What did you want me to do? Lay down and die?"

"Yeah! I kind of think when you break up with someone

they should just die."

She smirked. That was a funny, relatable take. He was always a good joke writer even in an emotional pinch.

"You are a child," she said. "Why do you even care about what I'm doing? You were in a fucking Adam Sandler movie."

"Yeah, I have an actual career to protect, Sophie."

There it was. The arrow that slayed her. He had an actual career - what she was doing was meaningless. He was just concerned she might get in his way. He knew she had no way for him to get in.

"I'm going back inside."

Matt grabbed her arm to stop her. She considered swatting it away, but she was always afraid he might hit her harder. He had never hit her before, but he was an angry guy and a strong guy at that.

"Okay, I'm sorry, Sophie. I am. But you really hurt my feelings."

Fuck this. She tugged her arm free.

"Are you seriously this delusional?" She stared at him as if he would answer. "You hurt my feelings. My reputation. You talked about me on stage and then went on podcasts and did interviews where you talked about how your jokes are about me. People know my name in connection to you. And I didn't dare say anything because I thought a relationship should be kept private and I didn't want to embarrass you."

"And now you have! So can you stop?"

"Are you going to stop?"

He didn't say anything. He sucked his bottom lip instead.

"Fuck you," she said.

"Sophie, you have to understand. I have an audition for a Comedy Central half hour coming up. I can't get rid of this material yet."

There it was again. His actual opportunities held up against her cute amateur comedy. She knew that's what he thought of her. Or at the very least - it was what he wanted her to think. He wanted her to be envious and bow down to his real success. Here she was refusing.

"You're a selfish piece of shit."

"And you're a spiteful piece of shit."

She smirked. He was hurt, which meant, in a small way, that she was winning this interaction. If she was winning this interaction, then perhaps she won the whole damn breakup. (She understood that to outsiders she did not win the breakup. He had way more money than her.)

"That's fine. I can live with that. I'm not giving up this material if you aren't going to give me the same kindness."

"Why?! It's not like you're going to become anything."

"Excuse me?"

The door opened, which let Sophie experience the warm air that was inside Cafe Mustache. Fred, Arnie, and Simon all came outside. They figured the two of them would be done, but all three of them stopped in their tracks when they saw that the battle royale had not yet ended. The two of them were still standing, jabbing each other.

Matt ignored them. His eyes were glued to Sophie's and there was fire in them.

"You're not going to amount to anything, Sophie. You're nothing special. You're a decent-looking female comic with decent jokes. You're fine. Yeah, that hurts, doesn't it? The truth is you aren't bad. You aren't great. You're just fine. Mediocre. To top it off you suck at networking. You weren't smart enough to do these jokes until I pissed you off. Even then! You're not original. You need me to propel your pathetic career. You're almost 30 and you're just going to be a washed-up Chicago comic doing shows in bar basements until the day you die, fucking young male fans of yours to feel wanted. So good luck with that. Good luck with striking gold trying to tear me down. I hope you feel really good about yourself knowing that your comedy only exists to hurt my feelings. Take care, Soph."

Matt turned around and walked up Milwaukee Avenue. She half-wondered where he was going. The train was in the other direction. He likely wasn't even thinking of that. He just wanted to make the dramatic exit in the hopes that he had the last word, that she was on the ground gasping for her last breaths.

Sophie tried not to show how much that affected her. How much that seeped down into her blood and made it freeze cold. How much she wondered if he was right. Fred put his arms around her. It was a nice solace, but certainly no cure for the ache now felt.

Am I really nothing? she wondered. It felt like those words had been planned. That didn't feel like an impromptu speech. That felt practiced or written out in a letter than he never sent. It was what he had been thinking for a long time. It was what he thought of her. She feared it was what so many people thought of her.

"Hey, Matt!" Arnie yelled after him. "You suck!"

Matt didn't hesitate and he didn't turn around. He raised a gloved hand and flipped him off. Arnie looked at Sophie for validation and she gave her dear friend a half-smile as she continued to digest Matt's words.

At the karaoke bar everyone was up on their feet singing at the top of their lungs. Sharing shots and shout-singing drunkenly until two in the morning. She sat pensively, feigning smiles, but she couldn't let herself get swept up in the fun. Matt's speech haunted her.

Was she really mediocre?

Mediocrity felt worse than being terrible. Being terrible or being great were feats. Those were memorable. But being mediocre...being just okay...being fine. Sophie didn't want to live like that. She didn't want to be forgotten that way.

Later that night Sophie and Fred were in her bed as they had been almost every night for the past week and a half. Fred was sleeping, but Sophie was wide awake, repeating the hurtful words. They only hurt because she was afraid they were true. She never felt like chasing fame, but she didn't want to spiral into obscurity.

Fred lifted his sleepy head. Without his glasses on, his brown eyes were actually really big. You could see his long, girlish eyelashes as he opened his drowsy lids to see if she was awake.

"Are you sleeping?"

"Can't."

Fred reached over the nightstand to check his phone. It was almost four in the morning.

"It's so late. Or early. I don't know—"

"Just go back to sleep."

He dropped his head back on the pillow like that was a command, but she was surprised to hear him murmur, "Want to talk about it?"

She shook her head, which he couldn't really see in the dark.

"I'm honestly okay..."

"Everything he said was wrong, you know." Fred said. "He was talking about himself. He's the one who's nothing special."

Sophie smiled softly to herself. Fred just knew. For a young dude, he had a good head on his shoulders. She felt like she didn't deserve someone as kind as him in her bed. She had always deserved the jerks, like Matt. She wasn't sure why. Being with Fred made her wonder if that was because she was a jerk, too. She was a nothing-special-jerk.

"I guess. I just - it really got to me."

"I thought what he was saying was ridiculous," Fred said. He rolled over to face her better, his head still firmly planted on the pillow. "Remember what he said about your jokes depending on him? He's the one who feels like he can't get rid of his jokes about you without sabotaging his audition. Remember that. He was projecting his idiocy onto you."

She nodded. She hadn't actually thought of it like that. Maybe his words sounded so practiced and precise because he had practiced them before...on himself.

"I guess that could be true. Still. It all makes me think."

"Well, I think..."

Fred trailed off. He never completed his sentence. She glanced over to find that he had drifted back to sleep.

"Fred?"

Nothing. He was fast asleep. Good. He deserved it. He deserved a lot of great things. She was beginning to wonder if he deserved someone far better - kinder, happier, more giving - than she could ever hope to be.

ELEVEN

When Debra asked Sophie to hang out, she was always honored. Really, when anyone who wasn't Arnie asked her to hang out, she took it to heart. She felt like she was difficult to be around and that she wasn't anyone's go-to girl. So when Debra texted her to have coffee, she was excited.

The two of them were waiting in line at Cafe Mustache, which was a hipster coffee shop during the day. It was an odd coffee shop. The coffee was fine, the tea was good, the kitchen was limited to gumbo and burritos, and the pastries were practically nonexistent. Still, it was a kitschy place with a lot of seating and very close to Sophie's apartment.

"This place looks like it's trying so hard."

"I always feel like I have to impress the baristas here," Sophie said as she eyed the blond dude behind the counter who looked like he surfed to work.

"I have to tell you something," Debra said in a very sudden tone shift. She was brimming with excitement.

"Hm?"

Debra looked at Sophie for a moment with wide eyes as if she had already told her the news. It was like she was saying 'ta-da!' but she hadn't said anything else.

"What? Are you telling me telepathically or—"

"I'm moving to LA!"

There is was. The move. THE move. It's the move every comedian thinks about doing in every city across America. Do I go to LA and really prove myself? Even if you go to New York, you have the LA decision looming over your head. LA was the retirement home for comedy. You went there when you were ready to completely cash in, knowing you'd likely be sun-drenched for the rest of your life.

"You are?! For real?"

"It's for real!"

Sophie hugged Debra impulsively. She wasn't sure if the two of them had ever hugged before, because Sophie wasn't necessarily a hugger. She liked hugs, but she never initiated them.

"I'm so happy for you," she said in their hug. Then she pulled away and asked in a kind of joking voice that was also semi-serious (like everything a comedian says): "Why? Why are you leaving me???"

Debra grinned. "I have to get work. Like for real. Tired of these winters and losing out to parts on the coasts. We gotta be on the coasts. I'm telling you that's the only way to make it. And I want to make it."

Sophie nodded. She had heard this all before, from everyone she had known all of these years who decided to move. It always felt exciting as she couldn't help but get caught up in a friend's journey. What will happen to them out there? Will success be immediate or will it be a very long slog? Will it come at all? Will they come back?

But it also left her with the bittersweet feeling of being left behind.

Too mediocre to move.

They approached the counter and Sophie said, "Two lattes, please. Small."

Debra fished out her wallet, surprised by Sophie asking for both of their orders. Sophie put her hand on Debra's.

"I got this! We have to celebrate your move!"

Debra put away her wallet. "You're too sweet."

"5.73," the barista said.

"Actually, do you have three pennies?"

Debra shook her head and brought the wallet back out, taking out her debit card. She gave it to the barista and said, "Here. Use this."

"No, Deb! Come on. You aren't Hollywood yet—"

"And neither are you, asking for pennies like that."

"I don't really care who pays me as long as you pay me," the barista with sandy blonde beach hair said.

Sophie handed Debra the five dollar bill she had and Debra took it, stuffing it into her wallet.

"I might have a job, though," she said.

"What?" Now Sophie was interested. *The mythical job.* The reason everyone wanted to make the move.

"Okay. Keep this very DL. A friend out there is an editor. He was working on a few shows like Walking Dead and then some new pilot a friend of his was making. Well, that show got picked up by TBS and they are staffing it with new writers."

"And?"

"And! He encouraged me to send a script over, so I did. They love it! We're meeting when I get there."

That was really incredible.

"That's incredible," Sophie said.

"Obviously nothing is set in stone and I'm going no matter what, but it's a way in! One foot in the door. That's all I need."

"I want an opportunity like that," Sophie found herself wistfully saying out loud. She instantly worried that she shouldn't have said that. It was embarrassing to let people know what she wanted, especially after they just dropped a big bomb like that. She felt bad, but Debra seemed unphased. Instead she asked:

"You want to write for TV?"

"Yes, very much so."

"I didn't know that."

Sophie was surprised to hear this, thinking that everyone just assumed that was what she wanted because, well, it was what she wanted. Then again, she never talked about what she wanted - even to herself. She felt like admitting it all was to admit being a failure for not doing it. Yet there she was, spilling to Debra like she never had before:

"I really do. I have a Broad City spec and a Simpsons spec and an original. The Simpsons one is very bad, but it's there—"

"Sophie! I didn't know any of this."

Sophie picked at her cuticles nervously.

"Yeah, it's not like we sit around and talk about dreams, I guess."

"No, we don't," Debra said. "But you have to say what you want. Otherwise how does anyone know to give it to you?"

"You sound like my mom."

"I feel like I'm every comedian's mom," Debra laughed. "Listen. I'll give you my friend's contact info."

"Oh, you don't have to do that—"

"That's how this business works! You can't just sit around and hope people will ask to read your spec. You have to take charge and talk to the people who have the jobs you want."

Sophie smiled.

"I just thought you were one of those 'I want to sell out Madison Square Garden' types of stand ups."

"God, no! Do I seem that delusional?"

Debra shrugged. "Everyone seems delusional. I'm the only adult in comedy."

"You literally asked me a month ago if a 401K is 'for when

you're a ghost'."

Debra laughed at her own dumb question that she had once asked in earnest as the barista held up the two lattes. When Sophie grabbed them he said, "You know, I've got a screenplay."

Debra hardly looked up from her phone, leaving Sophie to entertain this SoCal coffee-slinger.

"It's about slavery, but black people are in charge and white people are the slaves. It's a sci-fi dramedy. It's chill as fuck. I can print a copy if you want to read it. My boss lets me use his printer if I scrub his toilet."

"His personal toilet or the one here?"

"The first one."

Finally, Debra looked up, emotionless. She stared at the white barista while she said, "I sent you the info, Soph."

The two of them walked away snickering as they found seats near the front window of the cafe.

"Debra, you don't seem to understand," Sophie joked. "It's a dramedy. Meaning, there are *some* laughs."

"I do not have the patience to entertainment white ignorance. Not today, Satan."

They took a seat at a table by the window. Sophie checked her phone and saw that Debra did send her the contact info she was asking for. Amazing. She was a real friend.

"I really appreciate that you sent me that."

"No problem," Debra said. "Tell him you know me."

Debra took a thoughtful sip of her latte, so Sophie did the same. She was still in awe that someone genuinely wanted to help her with her career. Everything in comedy felt cut-throat and competitive. It threw her off her center to have someone care with a gesture like that. Even just passing her name.

"So hypothetically, would your new man come with you to LA?"

Sophie shrugged. This conversation was making her wonder where her future was. Should she seize opportunity like Debra and go? Fred was a new addition to her life - not yet something to make plans around. She didn't want to stall her life any more than she already felt she had for new men.

It was extremely difficult to not compare her life to those who had already left Chicago and feel that Debra would have a similar amount of success. She had known so many people who left for the coasts and had varying degrees of success. It was hard to see from social media posts who was actually happy, but TV appearances and shows with semi-famous people were more than most Chicago comedians could boast. It was something to envy.

"Well?" Debra asked.

"Oh, I don't know. It's still so, so, so new."

"Yeah, but he's a cutie."

She blushed as if a compliment to Fred was a compliment to her taste like a parent taking pride in their child's achievements that had nothing to do with them.

"I haven't really talked about moving. With him or anyone."

"Really? But you've thought about it, right? I figure you've got to be out the door soon, especially if you want to write television."

Sophie glanced out the window. She loved this spot in this coffee shop. She loved this stretch of Milwaukee Avenue. She loved this neighborhood. She loved this city. Why couldn't they create meaningful, successful lives in the Paris of the Midwest?

"I just wish we didn't have to leave Chicago."

"Yeah, but we can get ultra rich and come back and just chill here cause we're bosses. We'll be like reverse Oprah."

"That's the dream."

Debra leaned forward like she had a juicy secret to tell

Sophie. Her voice got soft and thoughtful as she said, "For the longest time, I worried I wouldn't be ready to leave here. Like ever. Then one day, I just was. I feel like I was ready yesterday."

"But this is home."

"Baby bird, it might be time to fly."

Sophie looked out the window to see a bicyclist almost eat it on a pothole. She always shook her head at the hardcore bikers risking it all to ride the snowy winter roads. She wouldn't see bikers fall on black ice if she was in LA. There would be no black ice.

But there might be career opportunities, not shows that looked like they would lead somewhere that they never actually did. No more spinning wheels. No more wandering into black holes.

"I think you're right. I'll think about it."

"But first we have to buy that barista's screenplay."

"Who knew slavery was so chill?"

TWELVE

There's something about being in love that no one romanticizes. Probably because being in love isn't particularly romantic. It's just plain nice.

Sophie didn't want to say she was in love with Fred because she wasn't sure yet. Love was also a changing feeling. She hated the weight people put on it. It moved. It changed. It was like a seed that continued to grow and blossom and branch. It was always evolving and becoming stronger and more beautiful - with enough nurture, of course. They certainly were nurturing their small start.

When she looked over at Fred washing dishes in his studio apartment she was full of brimming warmth. She felt like her infatuation was seeping out of her eyeballs when she looked at him.

He stood in his tiny apartment near 19th and Ashland - way far southeast from where Sophie lived, which is why she hadn't been over there much since they had started this little tryst - and she couldn't help but admire him. She loved looking around his teeny space and feeling all of his personality spill into those walls.

He was washing dishes when she snuck behind him to

open his refrigerator and take out a block of chocolate cheese he had bought on a whim from the market.

"It tastes like fudge!" he texted her excitedly when he bought it. She felt a pang of excitement when her phone lit up with his name to let her know a stupid, mundane text from Fred had arrived. To her they weren't mundane. They were all full of wonder.

She would hate to lose those texts and lose the ability to enter his Pilsen fortress. She would hate to lose it all just to move to a place with promises.

"Did you seriously just come in here to sneak eat cheese?" The two of them laughed as Sophie grabbed a chunk of the chocolate havarti with her blue-painted fingernails. She nibbled it like a raccoon on a scavenger hunt. He laughed, holding a wet plate, and shooed her away.

"Go sit down! Pick something for us to watch."

"You have to have some cheese first!" she said, offering the fudgy cheese like a gift.

He picked at it and the two of them nibbled it together like mice who found a forbidden treasure.

"This is so very indulgent," he said.

"I'm so glad you bought it."

"Well, I just thought to myself 'do you want to live deliciously?'" he said in a goofy, faux-accent that sounded like Tim Curry.

"Is that from something?"

"Yeah, the movie *The Witch*." He looked over at her to see if it registered anything with her. It didn't. "It's such a good movie, but that line made me laugh out loud in the theater. I was the *only* person who had that reaction."

"I haven't seen it."

He pointed to his grubby futon that looked like it had survived a few college moves to make its way to this two-room studio that was really impressive for someone this young to have by himself. She wondered exactly how much money he made, but she was afraid to really ask. The answer would probably make her feel bad about every job she had in her twenties.

"Sit down," he instructed. "We're gonna watch that."

She did it happily. She liked being playfully bossed around by him. It made her forget that she was older than him. He finished wiping clean a dish with his *I <3 NY* dish towel that she loved. She loved he had it. She loved that he had magnets on his fridge from different places he'd visited. She noted that he was missing Chicago and he said that he wouldn't get one from Chicago unless he moved. She liked that he wanted to be here.

She also liked that he lived far away from her so that his apartment was a destination. It was a journey to travel over here. She wondered if it ever wouldn't be worth the journey.

As she watched Fred wipe his hands clean, wearing a college hoodie that was once again too big for him, she focused on the slope of his Roman-shaped nose. She lingered on his lips. She wondered if there would come a day when she would be tired of these things. Would there be a day when she even hated them?

For the moment she couldn't imagine it. She could only imagine possible adventures together. She wondered when the day would come when they would be too sick to have sex and lay around together in misery as they watched bad TV and slept. She wanted to go grocery shopping with him, arguing over which kind of milk to get. Or what if they took a trip to meet her family? How would he act around them? Would he delight them? Would they take a bus trip to Montreal to meet his French Canadian clan? How much English would they speak? Would they speak in French around Sophie so she couldn't hear their harsh judgements on his American girlfriend? Would he get bored with her stories and would she doze off during his, wondering what the thesis was? Perhaps he would smile at her at a party as she told a story he had already heard a dozen times before at a dozen other parties. He would smile at her and remain invested to see what this new audience would think. He might even chime in with details that she momentarily forgot. Would he wipe her tears when she ugly-cried, letting snot get all over a Kleenex?

"What are you staring at?" he asked her.

What would their first fight be about?

"What are you thinking?" he asked in real time.

When would they finally say they loved each other? Would the day come?

She sighed, pursing her lips together as he took a seat next to her on the old futon. She looked at the stained cover.

"How much sex have you had on this thing?"

He laughed. "Come on. You don't want to know that."

She shook her head. "You're right. I don't."

"Really? It was that easy?"

"I've just been through all that before. When I was younger I wanted to know all these past details. Like that would make me know a guy better. But it really just made me miserable."

"That's just jealousy-fuel."

"Exactly. You get it."

"That being said, describe the penises of every man who has ever been inside you."

She picked up the throw pillow next to her on the futon - surprised that he had a ratty old throw pillow that looked like it was crocheted by a grandma - and threw it at him.

"Please don't do that," he begged. "Or just tell me they were all shaped like little ants."

"Ew."

She admired his girlish eyes and wondered if those were his mother's eyes. What was Fred like when he was young?

Her brain was scrambling with thoughts as if she was running out of time. She wanted to know everything before the sands in the hourglass ran out.

"You keep looking at me," he said.

"I like what I see," she said. "I was just thinking. Do you miss your parents?"

"My parents? Sure," he said. "Actually, it's just me and my mom. And my grandma. And my sister."

"So no dad?"

He shook his head. "Sometimes I wonder if he's out there reading my writing. I wonder if he misses me, but that would be impossible. He never knew me."

So there it was, she thought. That's the sad thing that makes him funny.

"You would like my mom," he said. "She's very...loud."

"So you think I'm loud?"

"No, it's that...she was always kind of this activist. Like so vocal about any injustice. Even the smallest thing."

"That's cool."

"It can be embarrassing sometimes." His eyes got faraway like he was watching a screen of memories somewhere else. "Like this one time - I had to have been about twelve or thirteen - our church decided that instead of raising money every year for school supplies for kids in need, that we would get a stained glass window."

"How are those two connected?"

"Exactly. My mom thought it was insane. She even interrupted mass demanding to talk about it."

"But I agree with her!"

"I know, and I do, too. But at the time? I was so embarrassed." Fred's face twisted, half smiling, like he was feeling himself cringe as a tween in the pews of a Catholic church in Quebec.

"She was always like that, though. And if I told her she

was embarrassing me she would lecture me about how you have to stick up for things you believe in because no one else will."

Sophie nodded. "I like that."

"Like I said - you'd like her."

"So, that's it, huh? I remind you of your mom."

He smiled a very toothy smile that opened up his whole mouth like curtains being pulled open to reveal a white stage. "Do I remind you of your dad?"

"No! My parents are just regular Midwestern folks."

"They're together?"

"Yeah, I'm a loser whose parents are still together."

He put an arm around her and rubbed her shoulder with his surprisingly strong hand.

"They're quiet people and in that empty-nest phase of their life where they're taking up new hobbies. It's kind of weird. They don't talk to me much anymore - especially since my sister is doing all the normal settling down and having babies stuff. I feel like I'm not part of the family anymore. Or that they started a new family and I wasn't there for the meeting."

Fred shrugged. "That's adulthood, right? You either start a new family by having babies or find a family with friends or work or whatever. You make your life."

Their eyes met and she felt her stomach swirling. For a moment she forgot about her ideas to move to LA and forge a new community of people. How could she go anywhere with someone like him in front of her?

"Has anyone ever told you that you're an old soul?" she asked.

"I'm just a sensitive weirdo," he said while blushing. "It's nothing too deep, really."

He picked up the remote and turned on his small TV that sat on the cover table he had pushed against the wall.

She curled up next to him, loving how warm he felt in his oversized sweatshirt.

Her toenail scratched his jeans. She felt like she was home.

It would be really hard to leave home. She was feeling herself push toward not wanting to leave Chicago - maybe ever - until Debra's words of encouragement ringed in her ear like someone pushing her gently downhill.

Baby bird...

"Hey - before we start the movie," Fred said. "I want to know what you're doing on Valentine's Day."

"Valentine's Day?"

"Yeah," he said kind of nervously. "It's in a few days and I wanted to see if you wanted to spend it with me. No massacres, I swear."

He remembered.

"I guess. I never really make any plans—"

"Of course not. I bet you're way too cool to care about Valentine's Day."

For a second she felt embarrassed that she had ever wanted to project that image. Here was Fred being endlessly uncool by caring about things. And it was actually making him seem cool. She had always been a girl that would denounce Valentine's Day and then feel pangs of disappointment when past lovers didn't do anything for the day. She hated admitting it bothered her. She hated admitting that sometimes she wanted to be loved in the most uncool ways possible.

"Here's the thing though," Fred was saying. "I've been waiting for a good time to tell you this, but February fourteenth is also my birthday."

"It is?!"

"Yeah, so I kind of want you to celebrate my birthday with me. If that's cool?"

She smiled.

"What do you want to do?"

"Have dinner with you."

I might move to LA, she wanted to tell him.

"Really? Combination Valentine's Day and birthday seems like a big deal."

He nodded. "It can be a lot of pressure. If you're up for it."

She kissed him. She actually wasn't sure if she was. What if she ended up breaking his heart? What if she let him down? She felt like breaking his heart was inevitable. They were just biding time until she decided to pursue comedy for real.

Unless, of course, she chose to stay mediocre. She could have a regular love life on this futon with after-dinner cuddling in her younger lover's studio apartment. Oh, how nice that sounded and oh, how unsustainable.

The following day Sophie visited Tally in her office. She found Tally on the phone at her desk, finishing a phone call that was about Sophie.

"Okay, thank you," she was saying. "You'll love her. I promise you."

She hung up.

"Well?"

"You're on call for the commercial."

"What does that mean?"

"If the person gets sick or catches on fire, then you're in. But you probably won't be in. That almost never happens."

"Which part? The fire part?"

Tally leaned back in her chair and stared down Sophie. Tally could really master a look that said 'let's get down to business'. There were times when Sophie wondered how good her agent actually was at her job - how much of her lack of success was on her and how much was on Tally - but when she provided that look, Sophie felt herself fall into line.

"So...you wanted to discuss LA. How serious are you about it?"

She had avoided talking about it for years because she didn't want to be all talk. Having this conversation was serious to her.

"Pretty serious. When is pilot season?"

"It's now," Tally said. "But you aren't missing anything. You could go out for a month or two try and it."

Sophie nodded. "I guess I'm just wondering, would I keep working with you or—"

"I've got you! If you are feeling on the fence, though, I really recommend going out there for pilot season."

"Yeah, that would be great."

"I mean, you'll probably end up staying forever. Everyone does. But it's a cool trick to get yourself to take the leap."

Sophie chewed her bottom lip, thinking about it. It felt right. She couldn't think of a reason not to try it. Even if it was just a month or two.

"You should do it," Tally said as if she could read her indecisive thoughts. "It lasts like three months. We can set you up with a buttload of auditions and meetings and you'll be juicing and doing yoga on the beach in no time. Oh, my god, Sophie. LA is going to do wonders to your hair. I promise you. You need that so bad."

Sophie touched her hair self-consciously.

"I'm going to think about it. But yeah. That sounds great."

Sophie got up to head out.

"My advice to you is that if you feel the need to do it at all, it probably means you are ready to try it. It's like anything else in life. If you are continually thinking about breaking up with your boyfriend, it probably means you want to."

"Is that last piece of advice for me or you?"

Tally laughed. "It's just a metaphor! Geez. But. Now that you mention it. What about Freddie?"

She shook her head. “That’s not your business, Tally.”

Tally grinned to herself like the Cheshire Cat of matchmaking. “You guys better be thanking me at your wedding.”

Sophie left the room to hear Tally calling after her, “You better let me make a speech!”

THIRTEEN

Sophie sat in a booth in the Beat Kitchen, a punk bar that had hosted Chicago Underground Comedy for years. She sat with her notebook open across from Arnie, who was doing the same scribbling in his handheld notebook as the show was going on in the showroom behind them. As she planned her setlist, a shadow fell over her notebook. She looked up. Matt.

"Hey."

"Hey..." Sophie looked around to see if anyone else was watching their interaction besides Arnie, who pretended not to notice Matt.

"Did you think about what I said at all?"

"Jesus. Are you serious, Matt?"

"Go away, Arnie."

Arnie just put his head back down.

"Oh! Yes, I did, and I've been meaning to tell you - fuck off."

Matt grinned.

"Okay then," he said. "I'm about to bury you onstage. Hope you're ready."

"I don't care, man. You know what? I'm gonna move to

LA."

A stillness abruptly came into the air. She felt like everything froze around her. She surprised herself by saying it, but it flowed out of her like a geyser.

"You are?" Matt asked.

"You are?" Arnie asked with more sadness than Matt. She shouldn't have broken the news to her best friend in this way. She looked at him and tried to gesture with her eyebrows that they can talk about it later.

"Yeah," she said. She looked back up at Matt who was towering over their tiny booth. "So do what you want. Say what you want. You're the one who is going to be - what were your words again - a washed up Chicago comic?"

"How are you leaving that sweet little boy you're dating behind?"

Sophie hadn't thought about that or anything. She hadn't brought this up to Fred and suddenly she became worried that one of them would which was irrational considering neither of them talked to Fred. But it wouldn't be beyond Matt to try and ruin that for her.

Matt laughed like a fucking villain. "That's what I thought. You know that will explode, right?"

"Don't listen to him," Arnie said. "Your decision is your decision and everyone who loves you will respect it. I know I do."

She feigned a smile at Arnie, but Matt just had to interrupt the small nice moment between two best friends:

"Or you'll do what you always do: put some guy's dreams before yours. Have you even told him you're moving? I'm sure the second he says he's not coming with you you're going to drop him. You're going to crush that boy's heart like you crushed everyone else's. Oh, and I hear he's like a real professional, too. So that'll be another fun roadblock to your success."

"Why are you such a piece of shit?"

Matt leaned back as if he was satisfied that he had pressed the right button that almost made Sophie cry. He had done his research on Fred and was going to fling all this shit in her face and then act like she was the pathetic one. He was the one who spent time asking about Fred so that he could guilt her about her decisions - whether she stayed or left - and dangle a broken heart in front of her. He was malicious. He deserved to be taken down by her onstage.

"I know you better than most people."

"That doesn't mean anything. It just means you can push my buttons."

"Sophie. I want you to do well."

It was insulting that he said that. It was even more insulting if he honestly believed it. This was not encouraging her to do well. All of this was trying to press her down under his weight while he rose to the top.

"Fuck off. No, you don't. You think I don't remember everything you said to me? You want me to crash and burn so you can dance on my ashes."

"No, that's not true. But what is true is that we're different. You want a balanced life and I want to actually be a successful comic."

"Oh yeah? What about Vivian? Is she willing to go on this ride with you?"

She was going to play his game and he wasn't going to like it. He played dirty, so she would, too.

"Yeah, she's supportive—"

"You're an idiot. You're like every other delusional male comic. They never want to go on this ride with us. You know that, right? The regular people - we think they're our fans, but they're only on this ride for a couple stop. She'll want off. Especially after you start making jokes about your relationship. We're in this alone. It's just about us and audience. No one else matters, right?"

Matt stared her down as if he was looking through her, as if she would evaporate in his gaze. She would hold her ground. She wouldn't apologize for pinching him where it hurt. Not until he did.

"Yeah. I don't believe you. Can't wait to catch up with you after a year to see you've moved Vegas to teach improv."

The crowd in the showroom was cheering. The first comic had just finished and Matt walked into the room to check on the lineup. She turned to Arnie and couldn't help but feel her eyes fill with tears. She blinked rapidly to make them stop. One escaped her barrier of long lashes and rolled mid-way down her cheek.

"You're crying?" Arnie asked. "I'm the one who's gonna miss the hell out of you when you leave."

"I actually wasn't sure about leaving," she explained. "Until I said it. Now it feels like I have to."

"Don't just go to prove something to your ex-boyfriend. Go because you really want to."

She nodded grimly. "I think I do want to. I mean…I don't know for sure. But I don't know what's left for me here other than the same old mistakes."

"Mistakes…" Arnie said.

She reached across the table and grabbed his hand. "You're my best friend and that's definitely not a mistake. It's a triumph."

Just then Maura Sampson walked by. Great. That's exactly who Sophie wanted to see while she was wiping sadness off her face. Maura passed by them and glowered down at the two of them through her annoyingly fashionable Warby Parker glasses.

"Are you crying?"

"Hello to you, too, Maura," Sophie said.

Maura looked between the two of them, but Arnie gave

her a stare that told her to get the hell out of dodge. She pouted on her way to the showroom behind them, walking through the swinging door and out of their moment together.

"I guess I can't blame you for wanting to leave," Arnie said. "You wouldn't have to deal with that bitch anymore."

"She's so mean to me and I don't know why!"

"Aren't women like that?"

"Oh, my God. Really? In 2018? You're gonna say shit like that?"

Arnie shrugged. He could be such a bro sometimes.

"I'm just a well-meaning guy who happens to be gay. I'm far from perfect."

He got up, ready to go into the theater.

"You haven't told Fred yet, have you?"

She shook her head.

"Like I said - I didn't know I was going to. I just said that and now it's like—"

"Don't."

"What?"

"Don't make yourself do something you don't want to do just cause you said you would to that asshole. I say I'm going to do shit all the time that I don't do. Honey, guess what? No one cares."

"I hate seeming wishy washy."

"You're allowed to make any choice you want for your life. And you're even allowed to change your mind about those choices. No one has to be you except for you."

She nodded, wiping away those tears that kept trickling down like babbling brook rolling down her face.

"Are you okay to perform tonight? You don't have to, you know."

She nodded. Of course she would perform. She had to. That was why she was there. That was why she did everything. She lived for comedy. It was her priority above family, friends,

Fred.

"Yeah. I'm a professional. Just cause I'm not laughing doesn't mean they can't right?"

FOURTEEN

It was the dreaded February fourteenth. Valentine's Day. A day that always held weight, even when Sophie pretended it didn't. It still loomed over the day like a lottery. *Maybe, even though I acted like I didn't care, someone would do something sweet. Nothing big. Just something simple and sweet. Maybe I'd be loved.*

She had the whole day free, but Fred was at work. She texted him happy birthday and he asked her to meet him for a nice dinner at a Wicker Park restaurant. She hadn't answered him to confirm. A few hours later she found herself walking to the beach in February. The sidewalks were full of slush and ice as she trudged in her winter boots to the shore just like she and Fred had done a month prior.

The past month had been a dream. It figured that she had to meet one of the most exciting people in her life as she was considering leaving her life behind and starting somewhere new. Fred felt like comfort food, like eating cornbread. He felt strong, homey, and warm. She wanted to end every night with him and see the sun bring out the flecks of gold in his brown eyes in the morning. She loved watching a room fill with early morning sun and brighten his olive-toned skin like they were being lit for a movie that only starred the two of them in his bed.

More and more she was going over to his studio so it could just be theirs. She loved feeling like they existed in a space that was just for them. Of course, it was his space and she was taking it over like water flooding a ship. She wondered if she would drown him soon.

Sophie always felt like she was too much or too little in relationships. Even early on. Yet Fred seemed grateful to be around her, a feeling that was brand new. As she walked all the way east on Armitage Avenue until she got to Lincoln Park, she flashed through memories of men who made her feel inadequate. Or the ones who were inadequate to her. These men had different spots throughout the city, as if she could map Chicago with memories of disappointment and weird sex, with some sweetness here and there.

She always felt like her biggest flaw was that she could be an idea. Men liked the idea of her. Look at this comedian in vintage clothes from the little shop she works at. Look at her onstage telling her silly jokes and making everyone watch her. Look at her confidence up there! Look how much she can make me laugh. Even my friends love her cause they are laughing at her jokes and she can hold her own with the guys. Look how much fun we'll have forever. I can even keep up and make her laugh sometimes—

And then it crashed, as it always did, when they discovered that she was a real person. She was a woman who had feelings and needs. She, like most comics, wasn't always "on". She liked to be serious off-stage. She liked to have alone time and long, quiet walks. She liked to show affection for people she cared about. She had demands like anyone in a relationship. She had ways she preferred to be treated.

That scared a lot of people. This idea somehow sprouted legs and feelings of its own? Pass. Onto the next thing.

Or it went the other way. They loved the idea of a quirky comedian, but they expected her to kind of settle down with them. Why did she have to go out every night? Was an open mic really necessary? Did she really have to do those shows? Did she really have to hang out with those horrible people? Wasn't this pursuit kind of gross? And so...they split.

Either way, she was tired of feeling like an idea. She was tired of being expected to give in and give up certain parts of herself. This was who she was. She wanted someone to like it. She thought she finally deserved it.

Fred seemed like he was that person, but perhaps he came at the wrong time.

She sat on an icy rock at the beach, thinking and look out into the nearly frozen water. Some winters it would get so cold that the lake actually froze. It would take nearly an entire summer for it defrost, making Lake Michigan too cold to swim in during the summer months.

How cold could it really be? she asked herself.

Sophie approached the shore, having a hard time telling the snowy sand from the frosted over water. It all kind of looked like an enormous white sheet that went out into the distance, blending into the gray winter sky. For a moment she felt like the only person in the entire city. It was just her on this white expanse, in this winter wasteland that turned into a vibrant city during the summer months. It was a city that she had loved for ten years. She wasn't sure if she was ready to break off this affair.

She tossed a rock into the lake, mostly to make sure the lake was there. She heard it plop down into the frigid water and disappear from her view. She then took off her boots, letting her wool socks feel the cold air around them. Then the socks came off. She rolled up her pants with adrenaline momentarily pumping heat into her feet. She walked into the water, just enough for the water to slowly lap at her ankles. It moved so slowly when it was weighed down by chunks of ice. It felt like it was energizing her from her toes on up.

Sophie remembered a story she had heard a long time ago about Christmas trees at the bottom of the lake. Seriously. There used to be a tradition at the turn-of-the-century that trees would be delivered via ship from Wisconsin or Michigan. The trees were brought down Lake Michigan and delivered to Chicagoans eager to decorate for Christmas. One ship, the Rouse Simmons, had an accident on its voyage to Chicago in 1912. On a terrible day the ship disappeared as it was overloaded with trees, so much so that the deck of the ship looked like a moving forest in the middle of the lake. Word was that the captain had overloaded the ship because he was in some financial trouble and wanted to sell as many as he could. There were about ten people onboard the ship and something like 5,000 trees. A storm hit and everyone went down. When the storm cleared, the Rouse Simmons had disappeared.

Legend had it that the trees sunk to the bottom of the lake and for decades full trees would wash ashore. Many of the trees that did were actually in perfect condition, because they had been frozen in the icy lake waters. A diver found the ship underwater in the 70's and it was still full of trees. It allegedly still was to this day. Imagine that. A forest of pine trees at the bottom of a midwestern lake.

She loved the idea of a prickly pine needle crossing her bare toes in that moment.

Instead they just started feeling prickly from the possibility frostbite that awaited her freezing toes. This was seriously so fucking cold.

She hopped out, suddenly certain of what she should do. Having experienced the coldest waters in the coldest Chicago months, she felt that she was ready for something warmer. Maybe water that didn't hold Christmas Trees captive under its currents.

Why not try it? she thought to herself as she desperately warmed her feet with her wool socks. She took off her scarf and wrapped her feet quickly, fearing that her toes might freeze.

But Fred. What about Fred?

No, she couldn't do that to him. She knew it wouldn't be right. She couldn't drag him into some kind of long distance relationship that he never asked to be in at the start of this. He'd moved there hoping to meet someone and have a good job and instead he met someone that would ask him to move somewhere else! No, that wouldn't be right. She couldn't do a long distance relationship. It wouldn't be right for *him*. Those always fizzled out or became an impossible romance filled with storybook expectations. She had to be more realistic and mature about this than he would. She cared so deeply for him already. She cared about every thought in his stupid head. Every word out of his mouth. Every silly headline he came up with. Every memory he chose to share. Every freckle on his back. Every beat of his heart when she laid in bed counting his heart like she was counting sheep, a metronome in his chest that lulled her to sleep.

She cared SO much about him, but she also cared about her career. She had been in a relationship with her career for much longer and she owed it to herself to see if she and comedy could go the distance.

Besides Fred was too young to know that this would go south if it were stretched across cities. It would strangle them both. Why make something beautiful suffer a prolonged death? She had to give this relationship a mercy killing, for both of their sakes. This would be good for both of them.

As she walked away from the freezing lake waters and back into civilization she took out her phone and texted Fred that she needed to talk to him tonight.

"Over dinner?" he texted back.

"No," she wrote. "Can you come over?"

FIFTEEN

Sophie opened the door to a worried Fred. She became suddenly aware that it was his birthday and it was Valentine's Day. Together, in one. She was so focused on what she felt like she had to do for herself that she forgot this was his big day.

Don't do this, she thought to herself.

"Hey, Sophie," he said with wild eyes. "I came as soon as I could. Are you okay?"

He kissed her, but she was kind of unresponsive. She wasn't sure how to go about this and the fact that it seemed so hard made her wonder if she was doing the right thing.

"What's wrong?"

You're about to become the most hated woman in the world, she told herself.

Fred took off his coat and tossed it on her couch. He was wearing the olive green sweater she gave him. It really did make the gold flecks in his eyes burn bright like they were being lit on fire. His eyes looked bronze, even though they were filled with concern.

Sumi was out on the town, having a Valentine's Day dinner with her girlfriends, something that Sophie thought was even dumber than Valentine's Day dinners. Standing in front of a concerned Fred, however, she didn't think either thing was corny. It was nice to be surrounded by friends and loved ones. Why the fuck was she trying to cut ties with people who wanted to spend time with her?

Is it really corny to care about people? she asked herself. *Jesus Christ, Sophie. Stop trying to be so fucking cool and above-it-all for one day.*

"Hey, Sophie. My mind reading skills aren't that good today, so you've got to tell me what this is about."

"Fred..."

She looked up at him, upset, with water filling up her lower lids again.

"Please don't say what it feels like you are going to say," he said. He looked so concerned as he tried his best at calmly reading her. God, he was even understanding during his own breakup.

She looked away, contorting her lips to try not to frown. Which must have just looked uglier.

"Sophie. It's...it's my birthday. I mean..."

She shook her head. "I know." Tears started falling down her face. She felt like a total asshole to be the one crying during a breakup.

"And Valentine's Day."

"Okay, well—"

"Sophie." He tried to meet her gaze, but she just couldn't do it. "Are you serious? Sophie. Look at me. You have to at least look at me."

"This just isn't going to work."

Fred sat down, which is when Sophie noticed that he had dressed up for this. He'd dressed up for his own heartbreak. He wore the sweater she gave him over a collared shirt that was tucked into corduroy pants. His hair was brushed out of his eyes and he was wearing contacts which made his eyes look huge like giant drains that were taking in everything around them.

Great. That was just what she needed. His enormous, darling eyes emoting every possible pain at her.

"Well," he said with his head in his hands. "This is shocking."

"I know. But—"

"Do you know, Sophie? You do know it's Valentine's Day, right? Like this isn't the holiday where you are supposed to prank people?"

"I have to—"

"You *have* to do this?" He softened the harshness in his voice, the need to make a caustic remark back at her to either lighten the mood or hurt her or both by following that up with, "Is someone making you? Sophie, are you being threatened by the Capone?"

He smiled as his eyes watered. She felt like those eyes were pulling out her intestines.

"Fred...the thing is..." She had no idea what to say or how to say it because she felt like she hadn't even fully articulated to herself why she was doing this. She was fumbling over her words like she was attempting to catch a football. "You're younger than me and you've only had one other real relationship—"

"That doesn't mean anything—"

"I just think you should go out and meet more people."

Fred stood up angrily. It was the angriest she had ever seen him, making her realize that she really hadn't known him long enough to know how he would react to this. That being said, even his angry wasn't that rage-filled. He felt sad and passionate, like an actor in an old French movie.

"What are you talking about? You're talking to me like you're my counselor."

"I just want what's best for you—"

"But you're my girlfriend... right?"

They hadn't really used those words. Boyfriend and girlfriend. They were just seeing each other. It was fun and casual. At least she thought it was. She thought that was what she wanted, but if that was all this was then why was it so hard to pull the plug?

"Fred, I don't know..."

"That's what you are to me. Did you know that? Did I need to spell it out and have some kind of archaic define-the-relationship talk with you? You're not just some girl I'm dating. Sophie, you—"

She couldn't let him go on. It was like he was clawing at her organs to get at her heart. It felt savage, desperate, and it was all her fault.

"You should explore your options, Fred. I'm the first person you've dated in this huge, new city."

"Fuck that! Do you hear yourself?"

"What—"

"Explore my options? I don't want to do that. Why should I date other people and be miserable knowing that I could be with you and be happy?"

"You don't know that—"

"I do, though." When he said it, she felt it. God, the *conviction*. The quiver in his voice as he defended his feelings. He believed every word he said. He really meant it. Sophie thought of the way he described his mother, standing up for what she believed in. She would be proud of her son if she could see him in her living room, laying out every injustice of this breakup before her to convince her that this was the wrong choice. And honestly? It could work. Sophie still didn't know what was right.

"Who are you to decide what's best for me, Sophie?"

But then again, she did. She had been here before. She knew a long distance relationship early on in this relationship wouldn't last. She thought it was impossible and she had had enough heartbreaks to know that he would get through this. You always got through it. Because you had to.

"I just know how this works."

"That's bullshit."

"I'm doing what's best for you."

"Let me decide for myself what's best for me."

"But if you end up breaking up with me—"

Fred threw his hands in the air. "Then that happens. I'd rather it be organic than forced." He bit his lower lip. It was as if he just heard himself and realized that he might be making a mountain out of a molehill. Maybe she really wanted this.

"Unless...I don't know. Do you really want to break up with me?"

She looked down at her socks. This conversation had her feeling like a little girl whose parents caught her in a lie and were making her explain herself.

"I don't want to break up with you. It just feels like I have to."

"According to what? I don't need you to make a decision on my behalf. I'm an adult."

"That's adorable."

"Sophie!"

Her jokes weren't welcome here and his tone really made him seem more adult than her. He was grasping to make sense of this and he was right to do so. It barely made sense. She sat down on the couch and he followed, sitting beside her and staring wide-eyed. His eyes seemed to beg her to change her mind. His eyes said 'you don't know what you're doing' and she wasn't sure if she did. She was afraid she'd change her mind tomorrow and make the whole thing worse.

"You're right. This is for me."

She still couldn't believe what she was doing. There was a voice in the back of her head telling her to turn around, to take it all back. While another voice was encouraging her, calmly, that this was right in the long-run.

"I'm projecting it onto you, but it's for me. I want to go to LA."

"This is all because you want to move to LA?"

"I have to for my career."

"Well, I didn't know you wanted to go. You've never mentioned it."

"It's all just been in my head."

He looked disappointed that there had been a conversation she'd had without him. "Do you really want to go?"

"I do. And you have to stay here. You just got here and it's a great place to be."

He reached his hand out to touch hers. She watched his large olive hand on her small pale one. She really loved his hands and she'd miss them so much even though she only had one month with them.

"I don't *have* to stay," he said softly.

"But you have a good thing going here."

Fred sat quietly for a moment, staring at their hands on top of one another. Neither one of them wanted to withdraw their hands because it might be the last time they touched. They couldn't be certain.

He didn't look at her when he suggested that they could work something out.

"Why bother?" Sophie said. "A long distance relationship turns into things that are gross. It would make us resent each other and..."

Fred waved his hand for her to stop, taking his hand away from hers. He looked like he was deep in his head, intent on figuring out a solution to this unforeseen heartbreak. But he also didn't want to push her away.

"Okay, I'll leave." He stood up. "It sounds like you've made up your mind without me. It's weird. I felt like we were on the same page this whole time, from the moment we saw each other at that party."

"We were."

He couldn't look at her now and it made her feel disgusting. Like a truly bad person. *Please just look at me, Fred.* But he wouldn't. He simply shook his head and reached for his coat.

"I don't know how you could say that."

"Fred..."

"I'm falling in love with you and you're leaving me. So... we weren't. We weren't on the same page. Have a fucking heart."

He buttoned up his peacoat and the act of him leaving really upset Sophie in a way she didn't anticipate. So did his sudden outburst.

"I do have a heart," she said, feeling a need to cover herself in a shroud of dignity. She didn't want to be the bad guy. She wasn't the bad guy. People like Matt - assholes like that - were the shitheads. She was doing something noble here. Fred just didn't see it yet.

"Can you please not say these things to me?" he said, exasperated. He looked at her sternly with watery eyes. "You can tell these things to your friends, but not to me. You don't get to act like this is good for me. On my birthday...I mean, Jesus, Sophie..."

She tried to stop herself from getting emotional, so she got mean instead.

"Ok. I can't wait to become an Onion headline."

He winced, looking like he was in so much pain from the jabs she attempted to fling his way.

"Don't do that. Don't get snarky. If you're sad, be sad—"

She talked over him. "What'll it be? Comedian Girlfriend Biggest Killjoy?"

It hurt so bad. The air in the apartment felt like it was a

fog of pain and he could barely look at her as she got snarky at him, during her own breakup spiel. It was so insensitive and so far from the woman he had gotten to know. Meanwhile Sophie could feel herself feel ugly to him. She could feel the effects of her self-sabotage.

"I would never do that to you," he said. And then he added, "And that's not a good headline."

It should have made her crack a smile. Ordinarily it would. But they were both too sad and tense to let levity in.

"We both essentially do the same thing, you know. We both exploit our pain for humor, so don't act like—"

He turned to her abruptly. He was actually mad at this point. He was mad at her for suggesting he would use her for humor and she didn't seem to understand why.

"I can't make you see that I'm not like every other vindictive asshole you've ever known. You have to see that for yourself. And maybe you're the one who destroys your own happiness, but I think you're a lot more than that. I think this could be the time you don't do that. You can choose not to do this, you know? You have to get out of your own way."

She had nothing to say. Nothing funny or witty or smart. Nothing sweet or nice. She felt utterly deflated.

"You think you're doing this for me, but it's all for you."

"I know," she said.

"Don't make up some lame excuse about my feelings or my youth. This is all about you and I really hope that you get out of your way enough to make this decision worth it."

"That's why I have to move to LA."

She tried to muster a strong face, but she couldn't. Her face was wrinkling with tears that flowed down to her mouth and dribbled off her cheeks. She was aware of how ugly she must look in that moment and hoped it would make this easier on him.

But there she was again, thinking it was all for him,

when it was really all for her. Every single second of this conversation was for her.

"You know, Sophie...no one is perfect. No one will fit into your life perfectly. People have to make concessions."

"No, I wouldn't ask you to do that."

"Ask me to! I want you to ask me to."

"That's not fair."

"You just don't want to."

He slammed the door behind him. Then opened it again and peeked his head in with his cheeks flushed red in anger and tears. She couldn't believe he was so freely crying.

"I'm sorry. I didn't mean to slam the door. I'm shutting it now, all regular-like." He was charming and cute even when his heart was broken. His head disappeared in the crack and he shut the door super quietly and slowly. It shut so slowly that Sophie hoped he would never shut it at all. She hoped he would leave it open for her to change her mind.

When it shut, it shut for good. Sophie was left standing in the living room of her apartment while the rest of the city celebrated love and friendship. While Fred cried off his 24th birthday. She was left to face her dreams and ambitions alone in her apartment, the way she thought she should.

All she wanted to do was sob.

If you're sad, be sad. His words rang in her ears. She was feeling really *really* sad.

She changed into pajamas and got into bed by herself. It was super early still, only about eight. She rarely went to bed before midnight, but her body felt sore, like she had just ran a marathon. There was no way she would fall asleep even with the aid of crying her eyes out.

She laid in bed for a while, staring at the ceiling and hoping to fall asleep, but Fred's lullaby was keeping her up.

"If you're sad, be sad," and "You have to get out of your own way."

Am I in my own way? she wondered. *If going to LA is getting ahead of myself, then why do I feel so shitty?*

All she could do was replay the night, from the moment he got there looking dressed up and dapper to the wide-eyed sadness he left with. Every line replayed in her head like she was rewinding and rewatching the footage. She kicked herself for sounding mean and sarcastic when he was clearly in so much pain. She kicked herself for doing it at all. *Why today? Of all days? What is wrong with me?*

She was keeping herself awake with these scenes and questions that only made herself feel worse. *God, fuck this. Fuck this. I did what I did.*

Laying in bed all night wasn't going to make anything better. She didn't get to be the bad guy *and* feel good about herself, so all that was left was forcing herself to forget. Time would heal this wound eventually, but in the meantime she had to do *something*. Luckily, she was in the perfect line of work for that. Her whole job was to make jokes and get drunk while she helped people forget their problems. Shouldn't she do that, too?

She picked up her phone and texted Arnie. "U up?"

He responded almost instantly: "New phone, who dis?"

The corners of her mouth felt weighted down, so the best she could muster was a weird half-smile at Arnie's joke. *This is what friends are for.*

He wrote: "We're at Gallery Cabaret. Come on down!"

She got out of bed, changing back into her day clothes.

SIXTEEN

Sophie walked up to Gallery Cabaret, an artsy dive bar that was covered in murals and graffiti art. She paused before she really got to the doorway to check her phone. Maybe Fred had reached out to her.

Nothing.

She saw an older comedian, Jack, who stood outside of the bar smoking. God, that guy had been in the comedy scene forever - probably almost as long as she had been alive.

"Sophie Martin!" he said in throaty voice as she put her phone away. "I see you!"

Sophie nodded at the hodgepodge group of comics outside the bar. She only really recognized Jack, so it was possible the others were regular people, but comics had a look about them. Flannel shirts, bearded, thirsting for validation. That kind of look.

"Hey, Jack! Long time no see."

"Yeah, well, I got sober!" Jack said. He then lifted his cigarette. "So I started chain-smoking."

"Oh. Good trade off?"

"It's great! No more late-night delivery I can't remember ordering," he said jovially. "But I started coughing blood. Is that serious? Should I be worried?"

Sophie pat Jack on the back.

"Nice see you, man. I'm glad you're back."

She opened the red door to enter the dimly lit bar, but could hear Jack's jolly and smoke-filled voice call after her, "Hey, I'm always here. I'm like a ghost. Can't stop haunting the comedy scene. Boo. Hahaha, like a ghost, right? God, I'm sad."

She laughed to herself at his self-deprecation. Sometimes she wondered if she shouldn't laugh when a peer made a joke like that. She wondered if she should call out their pain and ask if they needed help. She wondered if comedians were all too often enablers, not for the sake of the art and the love of the joke. No. But because they all thought that someone else could help their career and being the buzzkill meant killing off your own chances at success.

She stepped inside where she immediately spotted Arnie, Debra, Simon and Maura - why fucking Maura? - sitting at a booth together near the door.

She slipped into the booth and let everyone look her up and down.

"You look like shit," Simon said.

"Finally," Maura said.

She ignored Maura and sat down. She realized she probably did look bad. She hadn't tried at all. Usually she put on her lipstick, but not tonight. She hadn't even washed her face. All she did was change into jeans. She was even still wearing the dirty henley she wore to bed.

"Comedians!" Debra said while lifting her glass. "We're the shitty friends who might not be able to make your baby shower because we have a show in Kokomo, Indiana."

Everyone lifted their glasses to prepare this faux cheers. Sophie couldn't tell if they were starting this bit in her presence or if she had walked in one something.

"We're 'that friend'." Simon said to the agreement of everyone around them.

"We're the friend who you'll probably feel bad for in twenty years," Maura said. For once Sophie agreed with something Maura said.

"We're the friend who might be dead in twenty years," Arnie added.

Everyone laughed, then Debra added, louder, "Or five. I eat so much terrible bar food"

"I'm made of onion rings and beer," Simon added.

Jack walked in and walked right up to the table. "We're the friend who can't be trusted with a best man speech at your wedding because we'll probably make a lot of jokes that will ruin your wedding."

"Or the whole damn marriage," Debra said.

Every nodded in agreement. Arnie looked to Sophie to say something, so she did.

"We're the friend that will pretty much never have any major life accomplishment that isn't getting 200 likes on a status about dropping burrito rice down your bra."

"We're the friend who can't hold down a relationship," Maura said with a wink at Sophie. You know what? For once she didn't hate her so much.

"Here, here!" she shouted.

Everyone tapped glasses together, but Arnie looked at Sophie perplexed. He mouthed 'what' but she ignored him, so he said, "Sophie, you got a nice, normal guy, though!"

"You holding out on us?" Jack said.

"Finally. You're off the market. I can't get laid when you are single."

Nevermind. She hated Maura again. "Fuck you, Maura."

"Whoa, kitty has claws!" Jack yelled like he was about to watch a girl-on-girl mud wrestling match.

Fuck them. All of them. Sophie got up from the table.

"Stop it. All of you. Maura, I'm not fucking my way into the spotlight. That's not how I'm working. You want to get ahead, get funnier. Get nicer. "

"Chill out," Maura shot back as if she had no idea what Sophie could be talking about.

"No. I'm tired of it. It's bad enough to be a woman in comedy among a bunch of misogynists—"

"Hey! Ladies, calm down!" Jack yelled like some kind of 80's Andrew Dice Clay wannabe.

"You're such a bitch to me, Maura. Why cut each other down like that? For what purpose?"

Sophie looked at Maura, whose face remained nonplussed.

"Wait, do you want me to answer that?"

"I don't know," Sophie said as she turned away. "I don't know what I want." *Wait…did Maura have an answer?* It didn't matter. She didn't want to hear it. Whatever bitchy thing Maura had to say could wait. Sophie thought she could handle this tonight, but she was wrong.

She already missed Fred.

"We're all coping, right?" Debra said, watching Sophie storm out. "That's why we're doing this? Cool. Just checking."

As Sophie bolted toward the door to hide her face in shame after being so vulnerable with them Arnie shouted after her and followed her out. She felt like such an idiot. What was she doing getting mad at them? These were her friends and peers, her co-workers, and she just made such a mess in front of them. She always held her cards close to her chest around her peers and for good reason. She felt like whenever she let down her guard and got emotional, this happened. She exploded at people. She didn't burn bridges - she blew them up with dynamite.

Get out of your own way.

"Sophie!" Arnie said when he followed her out into the

cold. He wasn't even wearing a coat.

"What, Arnie? What now?"

"What now? Are you kidding me, Sophie? What's going on. Talk to me here."

She shook her head, trying to shake the tears that were coming hot into her eyes. Why was today so fucking full of crying? She felt like a child suddenly who would cry so hard that she couldn't breathe. She took a breath and tried to talk, but felt herself hyperventilate while fighting tears.

"I don't know. I just sabotage myself over and over again."

"Hey, it's okay. Just breathe."

Arnie put his hand on her back and patted it like someone helping a baby burp. Like someone trying to stop her from being so fussy. She paused and took a deep breath in. She closed her eyes and breathed out. With her exhale she felt herself talk like a tumble of feelings waterfalling out of her mouth.

"I don't want to be some disaster artist like Jack. A total burnout who doesn't know they should have quit comedy ten years ago. I don't want to be some scene-mainstay."

"Yeah, that's not you—"

"But I feel like it *will* be, Arnie. That's my inevitable future. I keep fucking things up, you know? It's like I can't help myself. Whether I'm dating the wrong people or holding myself back on stage or saying too much in a bar full of friends or telling the best guy I've ever known that we can't be together."

"Okay, so I'm guessing it's mostly the last one?" Arnie asked with raised eyebrows. Now that he knew what the object of her meltdown was, he felt better equipped to handle all of it. Seeing the knowing look on Arnie's face - as if he now knew which tools to use in attempting to help her feel better - made all of these feelings bubble out of her into one giant sob. Her head fell into her hands as she shook with sadness. Arnie opened his arms and took her in his wings.

"You need to stop blaming yourself, kid."

He pulled back, watching her cry affectionately. He looked at her like an older brother, or what she imagined an older brother did for his kid sister. But then he did something unexpected. He looked like he was going in for a kiss. She sheepishly smiled at him and his lips landed on her forehead.

"I don't know," he said. "I felt compelled to kiss you. I literally have no idea why. I haven't kissed a woman since I was sixteen."

"It's okay," she said, and she meant it. She thought literally nothing of it. Everything else felt like too much of a mess to worry about this one subtle almost-kiss. "We're strange, vulnerable, insecure people. I guess sometimes it's nice to show some damn emotion."

"I love you, dude," Arnie said and brought her in for yet another hug. This was the most they had certainly ever hugged. Being this close to him, she smelled something kind of rancid. It ruined the moment entirely, but she asked, "Did you fart?"

"Yeah, but be chill about it." He laughed. "You're always trying to weasel out of some real feeling."

"Haha, no, I'm not!"

"You are! We've never hugged this long."

"It's starting to be too long—"

"Just feel it out. It's okay."

And he was right. She knew he was right. She settled into the warm hug, relaxing her muscles into his chest. It was okay.

SEVENTEEN

The next night she was back on her grind. That was what comics called working. They were 'hustling' or 'grinding'. It was all very gross language - all kind of sexual or illicit like they were all working underground at their seedy jokes - but it described what she was out doing again. She was making jokes. She wasn't wallowing in her bedroom. She was at The Lincoln Lodge again, pouring over her notebook as she sat at the bar alone. She wasn't writing jokes, however. She was writing a pro/con list of reasons to stay here. After she broke up with Fred, she decided to throw herself into her decision to leave, to commit to it with 100% of her being. But even with that determination she was still so unsure. She wondered if she would ever be sure about the decision. Did she have enough money? Did she have enough contacts? Had she really exhausted all her possibilities in Chicago? Would she be leaving before a big opportunity would explode onto the Chicago scene?

"Wowwie. Two women on one line-up. Can you believe it?"

She looked up. It was Maura. Maura was wearing a tank top like usual to show off her colorful arms. Her tank read "feminist" across her small chest. Sophie had a hard time not viscerally rolling her eyes at the printed tank top. She wanted to splatter blood across her chest the way that PETA did to people who wore fur coats.

Cool feminist, Sophie thought as she looked at the cursive printed letters. *Maura is a fucking champion of women.*

"Hey. Maura," Sophie said, like she was entertaining a fly that just buzzed up to her. "I don't really have the time right now—"

But Maura wouldn't go away. She hovered in front of Sophie like a gnat, even craning her nosy neck to look at her notebook.

"Writing new jokes?" She saw the list of pros and cons that Sophie was working on. "Oh. I'm sorry. I didn't mean to look."

Yes, you did, Sophie thought and closed the notebook. Maybe Maura was the only reason she really needed for leaving this city.

"I'm sorry I looked at your notebook," she earnestly said, to Sophie's surprise. Maura sat down next to her in the weirdest act of semi-kindness that Sophie had ever seen from her. "I didn't know you were thinking about moving."

Was the thought of her leaving - of one less woman to "compete" with in Chicago - all that Maura needed to finally befriend Sophie?

"Kind of. I'm also thinking of not doing it."

"I can see that," Maura said with a smile. "Want to just flip a coin and get the decision over with?"

What was going on? Why was she being so...nice?

"No. I just. I don't know. You don't know me. I know you don't want to, but I feel...stuck. Or something. I don't know what to do."

"So go. At least for a little bit. You should try it."

"I want to. But am I making the right choice? Should I

leave? Should I stay?"

"You can't stay and become some kind of Jack Gemstone local."

So she was encouraging Sophie to go. Of course.

"I mean, I know you want me to go," Sophie said. "But what would you do if you were me?"

Sophie almost wanted to take back her question. She felt so needy asking her longtime nemesis for advice. It felt so gross. She felt like she was bleeding in front of her and asking her to find a bandage. Why would Maura ever help her? She figured Maura was simply waiting for the opportunity to pounce like a panther waiting to claw its prey.

But then she said, "Hey. You're great." She said it so sincerely.

"You hate me."

"No, I don't." Maura got quiet and looked away for a second. There was more to that. Sophie watched her face carefully, watching Maura gather the explanation for her behavior. She could actually see it in her face. She was weighing her options, doing her own pros and cons list, of whether she should tell Sophie why she hated her. Or, according to her, didn't hate her but just totally acted like it for years.

"What?" Sophie asked. "You look like you want to say something."

Maura met her gaze, her lips forming a straight pensive line. "I really don't hate you. I hope you know that."

"How could I?"

"I get that," she said. "I also get jealous of you. Because you're really fucking good and comedy still acts like there can only be one woman in anything, but I don't hate you. I actually...really like you."

"Funny way of showing it."

"Yeah, I suck," Maura laughed awkwardly. "I'm a weirdo. That's why I'm a comic..." That wasn't it.

"Yeah, we're all weirdos," Sophie said. She wanted to prod her for more. There was more.

"Um, also—"

There it was. There was more.

"This is really hard to say, but...I was kind of afraid of you because...I don't know...Matt."

"Matt? You mean his comedy about me?"

Her eyes got wide and worried. "No, no. Not at all." She looked really serious and scared. It gave Sophie a horrible, sinking feeling in her stomach. There was so much more to this and she could see it on Maura's face.

Oh, fuck. He didn't...

"You guys were dating and so I just assumed you really had his back and would never believe me or anything—"

There was the language. *Believe.* Nothing good comes around that word when a woman is saying it in relation to a man.

"What the fuck did he do?" Sophie asked as softly as possible. Rage was boiling inside of her and she didn't even know what he had done yet.

"It's no big deal, I guess," Sophie started to say. "It was just right before you guys started dating or maybe early on, I don't know exactly. We were at a party and...I don't know...this probably sucks to hear and I don't want to be a bummer—"

"Maura. You're not a bummer. I need to know this."

"Do you, though?" Her question was so weird. Of course? Shouldn't she know?

She nodded. She thought it would be irresponsible to refuse this information now and she had a bad feeling about what was coming. A pit formed in her stomach for all of her organs to fall into. She had a feeling she knew what she didn't know.

"I never wanted to tell you because I didn't know where

you stood on him. Even if you guys were broken up or something, maybe you would still defend him—"

"I wouldn't—"

"—Or think I was a crazy bitch or something. So I just never knew how to act around you. I think I acted like a crazy bitch because I was scared. I always associated you with him. It was really hard for me to not see you as, like, his appendage or something."

"Oh, God. I'm sorry. I really am." Sophie felt like shit for being associated with him at all if he did something to her. She had no idea. How could she know?

"I was passed out cause I got too drunk and fell asleep in a pile of coats at a party and I woke up to him fondling me. He had a hand up my dress…it was…I smacked him away and started shouting at him and stormed out of the room."

"Oh, my God…"

"Yeah, but it's not like he really did anything. He didn't rape me."

"He assaulted you."

She shrugged sadly. "Yeah, he did. I just didn't know how to say this ever. To anyone."

"Wait. Does no one know?"

She shook her head. "And now he's getting more and more successful."

"But with the Me Too Movement, people will want to know. They're more aware of how to deal with this kind of thing."

"Come on," she said, looking Sophie dead in the eyes. "Do you really believe that?"

No. She was right. Sophie knew she was right. People still didn't care.

"The pendulum is already starting to swing back the other way," Maura said to fill their haunted silence. "The abusers are, like, making their comebacks already. It's insane!

If I spoke up against Matt, it would just be washed out immediately. I don't think anyone would listen to me."

Sophie nodded. That was probably true. Sophie wasn't sure if she would have believed it. If she had been Matt's girlfriend at the time she heard this...she probably would have said Maura was lying. Knowing that about herself made her want to vomit. What the fuck was wrong with her for being with that guy? And what was wrong with her for maybe taking his side without even realizing she was?

It felt selfish, but all of this made Sophie wonder what it said about her that she kept Matt's company for so long. What did that mean about her judgement of people that she had no idea?

"Besides," Maura added. "I already know what they would say. 'It wasn't that bad'. That's the weird thing about these conversations. People always seem to want them to be way fucking worse. Like they'd only believe me if I had been murdered."

"At least then you'd be the star of some exploitative true crime documentary," Sophie joked, unsure if it would be appropriate.

Maura laughed. "Ah, stardom is only a death away." She wiped a tear from one of her eyes as she laughed and said, "I'm sorry, Sophie. I thought maybe you knew this."

"I really didn't," she said. She didn't. But now she wondered if she did, if there wasn't some kind of weird hint. "I just selfishly assumed you hated me. See? That's where my brain went. It's all about me!"

"We're both total weirdos."

"Maybe I'm *too* weird to do comedy."

"You're too weird and I'm too damaged," Maura said.

"Yeah, maybe." Sometimes it felt that way. As women in comedy, it felt like there were only so many boundaries they were allowed to break until they weren't allowed into the boys club that was standup. They still had to be ladylike and sexual objects even when joking about gagging from blowjobs. It felt like they still had to turn them on while not getting in the way of their paths to power. Be good girls. Shut up and take the jokes. Be the butt of their jokes. Don't speak up too loud.

"I hope you really don't think that, though," Maura said.

"Sometimes I do."

"No, I'm not too damaged or weird and neither are you. We have to keep going. Even if Matt and other guys like him - worse than him - are out there thriving. We have to thrive, too. We have to thrive harder."

"We have to do everything harder," Sophie said with an eye roll.

"Here's my belief: you have to take risks. If you don't, you'll always wonder. Right? Like there was some weird quirky dude I met at a party when I was in college who was obsessed with me and asked me to go on vacation with him for a summer. But I barely knew him. So I said no."

"Yeah, cause you didn't want to get murdered."

"He invented Groupon."

"So?"

"So what if we fell in love and got married and I got all that sick money?"

"Isn't that company failing really badly now—"

"That's beside the point."

"Okay, but what if you went on vacation and it was miserable."

"Then it would have been miserable. Then I would know. That's my point, though. If everything goes very wrong in LA, then you can come right back here and we'll all forget you ever left."

"Promise?"

Maura put her hand on her chest as if she was about to

say the Pledge of Allegiance.

"Scouts honor. You would be able to come home at any time. If I had gone on that vacation and it was horrible, then I would have been able to come home."

Maura took out a quarter from her pocket.

"How bout that coin toss?"

Sophie nodded. "All right."

"Heads is LA. Tails Chicago...or New York?"

She hadn't even really considered New York. She just knew she wouldn't dig it. The people, the way the city smelled of urine after it rained, the expensiveness of it all. The flashiness that rode down trash-filled streets. She couldn't get behind such blatant class struggle.

"No, I hate bagels," she said. It was true. Too bready.

"Oh god. That's sacrilege. Okay. Tails is staying. Heads is going."

Maura flipped the coin. They watched it launch into the air and fall down as if it were as graceful as a feather. It spun as it landed on the bar and came up heads. They looked at their result - a disappointing big reveal. It was, after all, just a coin. And yet it felt so definitive.

"That's that."

"It sure is," Sophie said. Tears welled in her eyes. God, she'd been crying so much lately. What was wrong with her these days? "Best out of three?"

"Are you going to cry? Maura asked.

"Maybe!"

"Oh, my God. You don't have to live your life by a coin—"

Sophie felt compelled to hug Maura. So she did. She wrapped her arms around her even though Maura wasn't expecting it and squeezed her. Maura's arms were down at her side and remained there for a second until she lifted one of her hands and patted Sophie's back. Sophie still couldn't tell if she was being genuine or just placating her. But it felt good.

Maura pulled back and looked over Sophie's shoulder. She was looking up, solemnly. What was she looking at?

"I've been added to this lineup, too."

Matt. Matt was behind her. Why did he keep sneaking up on her in a city he no longer lived in?

"Oh, cool. That's not awkward for everyone," Sophie said.

Sophie turned around and looked at him with daggers in her eyes. Not today. Not after the conversation she just had with Maura.

"God, why are you still here?" Sophie asked.

"I'm leaving next week. I've been filming a project with Joe Swanberg, so."

"Who fucking cares," Maura said. Hey, Maura wasn't half-bad. Sophie was really liking Maura now. It was a total 180.

"Sophie, can I talk to you alone?"

He had asked her to talk about three times now and each time it was terrible. She was tired of seeing his face whether it was in front of her or on a billboard. She was so sick of him and she was so sick of the way she let him ruin her day. She wanted to glide above his tall, horrible body and fly into the air to leave him behind in her dust.

She looked at Maura, who was stonily staring at Matt. If looks could kill, Matt would have melted into a puddle under her fiery gaze.

"It's funny how you always want to talk, but nothing gets done," Sophie said.

"I want to talk about our material."

Our?

"Our shared material?"

"Come on." Matt had a short fuse with her these days, but perhaps even he could hear his tone because he then added, "I've thought a lot about what you said and, well, I'm really sorry for what I said."

Sophie packed up her notebook and brushed past him to walk anywhere that wasn't right in front of her. "I gotta go onstage."

He reached out to grab her like he had that one day in front of Cafe Mustache only weeks ago, but he stopped himself. His hand hovered in the air, learning its own lessons.

"Stop using comedy as a weapon against me."

She stopped. Her feet planted powerfully on the ground as if she might sprout roots and become an oak tree in the middle of the theater. She felt it necessary to ground herself in front of his tornado of bullshit.

"And how are you going to use it?"

"I want to give up the jokes."

"I'm not even talking about the jokes anymore."

"No, I'm serious. I'm going to try new stuff tonight. Let me know what you think. And maybe you'll want to do the same?"

"And will you use your comedy as a weapon against women?"

"What?"

"Are you still taking advantage of women or was that a one-time thing right before we dated?"

He looked around. Maura had left the bar. She wasn't there to see this confrontation, which was probably for the best. It may have made her feel uncomfortable or worse, in danger.

"What are you talking about." He asked it flatly. Like it wasn't a question. It was a command to stop talking.

"I heard a story about you taking advantage of someone passed out at a party. Do you know what I'm talking about?"

He shook his head, looking at her like she was crazy. Except he wouldn't meet her in the eyes. It was like he was looking past her.

"You don't remember a girl passed out on a pile of coats

at a party and you had one hand up her skirt? You don't remember this?"

"What is this—"

"So how often did you do this to people that you don't remember the one time I heard about you doing it? Are you really that much of a fucking sicko?"

"What is this?" Matt said. "You heard one rumor and you're going to believe it?"

"I don't think it was a rumor..."

Matt clenched his jaw. "Of course this is the tactic you take."

"Tactic?!"

"You're so fucking jealous of me. Now you're going to MeToo me? Really?"

"You egomaniac."

"This is pathetic."

With that, he walked away. He gave himself the final say - which she hated - but he hadn't actually defended himself. He hadn't done much of anything at all. Was the ball truly in her court now? And she hadn't realized it until that moment, but was that a repetitive pattern of Matt's?

Or was he telling the truth? It felt fantastical now to think of a time in which she once trusted him.

She needed to go for a walk. She felt tears well up in her eyes, a too familiar feeling those days. Why was this so upsetting? Matt had assaulted Maura, someone that Sophie had badly misjudged. He was the bad guy. So why did that upset Sophie?

And how did she not see or hear about this before? Were they any signs? Did he do it to other people? Had people seen her as his ally, as complicit? Was she complicit?

She stood in the hallway that led to the showroom and cried. It just came out of her like a faucet turned on.

Why was this so upsetting...?

This isn't your trauma, she told herself.

"Hey," a voice said down the hall. It was Maura. Again. "Are you okay?"

Sophie shook her head. "I'm so sorry."

"You can do what you want," Maura said as if Sophie hadn't said anything at all. "But if he's mad at jokes you are making about the relationship he had with you, then he should have treated you better."

Maura was right - in theory. Sophie always felt that way. Things that happened to you were your stories to tell. That's why she didn't love doing jokes about celebrities - they were affecting her directly. But she also didn't want to unfairly tell a side of the story that hurt someone else. Even if it was true.

"I'm not trying to hurt anyone's feelings or be complicit to anything he does. I-I really didn't know," Sophie said. "I'm just trying to make strangers laugh."

It sounded venerable, even heroic to say that. But it simultaneously felt so stupid to act like telling jokes was honorable in some way. They were just making people laugh. They were just telling jokes. They weren't saving the world.

Maura shrugged.

"Like I said, do what you want. But everyone has been through this."

"I haven't," Sophie said. "And I didn't know you had."

"I'm not talking about that."

"What do you mean?"

"I'm talking about your jokes. That's the thing he's really mad at."

Sophie wiped away her tears. Maura didn't want to talk about her trauma anymore. She had told Sophie and was ready to move on. She certainly didn't want to rehash it with Matt.

"I have family that won't talk to me anymore after seeing my stand up."

Sophie's family had always been fairly supportive. Granted, she rarely told glaringly bad jokes about that. She talked about her parents' quirks or her sister's wedding, but nothing that any of them would object to. Her entire family knew that things they did were fair game for her act and they all had a fairly friendly Midwestern attitude about her comedy. It was all fun and games to her parents who were actually pretty proud of her, even if they were often wrapped up in themselves.

"Really? Why?"

"My family hates me joking about my pervert grandpa, but you know what? If they don't want me to tell those jokes then he should keep his thoughts about my boobs to himself."

"No kidding."

Maura took a swig of her mixed drink. "Cut me out of the will for all I care."

For the first time ever, Sophie admired Maura and the picture of this bitchy girl who hated her was finally coming together. Maura was protecting herself against her and against everyone. She was just kind of a bitch, but in a good way. She was a bitch in the way in which she got what she wanted because she knew it was what she deserved. Sophie felt she had misjudged her for the last few years.

"But how do you deal with telling those jokes knowing that they hate it?"

Maura pursed her lips together as she thought about it, "Well..." she began, swirling her strong around in her glass and following the little whiskey coke tornado she made. "It's rough, but these are our experiences. It's what we do, you know? We joke about things that happen to us, people we know, et cetera. It's how we cope with bullshit. Any joke that anyone has ever laughed at was inspired by something true."

"You're right." But...there was still a but. She still felt a tug at her heart telling her that there were exceptions. "But still. I don't want to hurt anyone."

"Even your shitty ex-boyfriend who was actively trying to hurt your reputation?"

"Yeah. I don't know. At the end of the day, these are just jokes, right? Jokes don't keep you warm at night."

"I wish they would." She took another long sip, almost finishing this entire drink before the show.

Sophie pulled out her pen and notebook. Maura looked over her shoulder to see that Sophie was writing out a set list that didn't include the jokes about Matt.

"Suit yourself," Maura said. "I'm gonna tell my pervert grandpa joke til I die. Or he dies. Whichever comes first."

The lights flickered and the audience were taking their seats. Maura and Sophie walked back into the theater to see that the place was pretty packed with people filing into the comedy club to laugh for an hour. That's all they wanted. They didn't care about jokes offending other comedians or family members. They figured most of the jokes the comedians told her embellished or made up entirely - and a lot of them were.

They don't know me. They don't know Matt. It doesn't matter to them

Matt knew that when he had talked about her. He knew the audience didn't care, but she'd always suspected that he didn't tell those jokes because he thought they were funny. He didn't tell them to entertain the crowds live in front of him or on American televisions and computer screens. He told them to hurt her. He told them so other comedians and those in the industry would ask who the joke was about and hold the stigma against her. She felt this was true in her heart. It was vengeance and now she was taking vengeance on his smear campaign.

Sophie left the theater to go to the bathroom, but as soon as she exited the double doors she ran straight into a familiar face. A long face with oval glasses and messy hair. A face that was sporting a bit of a sadness beard. It was Fred.

"I've been looking for you," he said.

She didn't know what to say. She wasn't expecting seeing him at all, so her mouth dropped into a perfect circle and "Oh" fell out.

"I want to talk, if you can."

There was the difference between Fred and Matt, yet again. Matt demanded they talked. Matt demanded Sophie listened to his every whim while Fred asked if it was convenient for her.

But what were the odds they'd both do this in one night? Jesus, she had to get out of this town.

"Everyone wants to talk."

"Sophie, please?"

"How did you know I'd be here?"

Fred smirked like she had asked a cute and insane question. "You post about all of your shows on Facebook."

Oh, that's right.

"I'm a disgusting self-promoting monster."

She forgot that he was easy to talk to, that the first night they met they bounced quips with Screwball speed.

"Can we talk?" he insisted. There was such an urgency in his eyes as if he feared this would be their final conversation.

"No, I really don't want to. I'm sorry. I have to go up tonight—"

"You don't want to talk?"

She took a deep breath.

"No."

Fred nodded. He then reached for her notebook that was in her hand. She didn't expect that move at all, so she didn't know to keep a tight grip. What the hell was he doing? He pulled out a pen from his pocket and began writing on an open page.

"Hey! What the—"

Fred scribbled quickly, likely fearing she would grab the notebook back. He held it up in front of her and it read: Maybe we can write then?

Again, a question. Not a statement. He was always asking if she was okay. She really liked his warmth and consideration. And she liked this stupid, clever trick.

She grabbed the notebook back, considered pocketing it and walking away. But instead she took his pen and wrote: *What's this about?*

Fred's brown and gold eyes flickered. He took the book back and hurriedly sketched some barely-legible chicken scratch. She watched him nimbly write, her eyes glazing over his intense face and large hands. Hands that she missed. She missed him.

He handed the notebook back to her. It read: *I miss you. But also I have a plan. Wanna hear it?*

Her face scrunched. A plan. She wasn't sure that she liked the sound of 'having a plan'. It sounded diabolical. He watched as she wrote back: *I don't have time right now.*

She handed it to him and his face fell as he took the notebook in his hands. He nodded and closed the notebook, handing it back to her with sadness weighing down his entire face. She felt horrible.

"Wait. Fred. I don't like big gestures. Or speeches, or—"

He shook his head. "I don't have those. I just have an idea. That's all."

He turned to go, taking this elusive idea with him. She felt her heart tug with him. She had always hated anyone fighting for her. She was a loyal lover, but when she made up her mind to end things she cut all the strings. Thus the pain. Thus the jokes and song and stories about her. People didn't like a closed door. They were used to doors with cracks in them, but she was never that way.

Sophie had broken up with people before. She had done

it a thousand times. But this one felt different. It felt like she hadn't given it a chance and that she should have given it a chance. This time she should have left the door ajar.

"Fred," she said to his back. "Tomorrow."

He turned back around to face her.

"Tomorrow?"

"Yeah. Meet me."

"At your house...?"

She shook her head. No, not there. Not any place where they had already said goodbyes. She wanted them to meet at a place where everything felt infinite and possible for the two of them.

"No. Someplace special."

She wanted him to know the place. It would be like a sign to her. If he knew it, maybe they should give this a chance. If he knew it, maybe he did know her.

She could tell he was confused, but he also loved this little lifeboat she was tossing to him.

Then came an overwhelming desire to embrace him, but she wondered if that would be cruel. What if she hugged him and then discarded him? What if she took him in for shelter and threw him out to the street in the middle of the night? She was planning on going to LA - she really felt she should - and she was terrified of hurting him with her departure.

They looked at each other and he gave her a soft smile, clearly not wanting to walk away from her. She did have to go to the bathroom, though. So she leaned in and gave him a kiss on the cheek before walking away quickly and disappearing into the bathroom.

EIGHTEEN

Sophie wondered if Fred would be able to find the "special place". She wondered if she even knew what that was. When she said it, she didn't actually have a place in mind. The beach? The Second City steps? The bus - which bus?

She hoped it would just come to her. And come to him, too. She wished he would text her and say "the blah blah blah, right?"

What am I doing?

Still, with no place to go, she couldn't stand still. She couldn't stay home knowing she would hurt Fred more than she already had. This left her wandering around Chicago on a kind of goodbye tour. She put on her worn pair of Saucony gym shoes and began her long walk, starting first in her own neighborhood. She wandered through her beloved Logan Square, mentally kissing every detail goodbye.

She walked up to the large monument in Logan Square, a white column that stood tall with an eagle perched on a Grecian-style podium. It was long and intimidating, European-looking in the middle of a traditionally Hispanic neighborhood, while being welcoming to anyone looking for a sign that they were in Logan Square. That they were home.

She looked up at that eagle and waved.

A man on a bench watched her wave and he smirked to himself. She instinctively wanted to say "what the fuck are you looking at?" But this was Chicago, not New York. You didn't say those things here. You thought them and pushed them all the way deep down inside, bottling up all your frustrations. Maybe that's why there were so many serial killers in the Midwest.

She thought these things as she made her way down Milwaukee Avenue, which cut through the neighborhood like a hipster mainstreet filled with craft bars, coffee shops and condos that were displacing hardworking families. The neighborhood changed more and more as she walked, with old diners being replaced with juice bars. Perhaps it was time for her to be replaced as well.

She followed Milwaukee Avenue down to North Avenue. This six cornered intersection - not *the* six corners, as true Chicagoans insisted that one was in Portage Park, but still one of Chicago's many six cornered intersections - was always such a jumble. It reminded her of Brooklyn, with bustling hipsters, tourists, families, and partiers all together. It was probably the busiest intersection in the city, or at least the most lively in Sophie's opinion.

A biker whizzed down Milwaukee and didn't want to slow down to a stop. They had to beat the coming yellow light and when they did this they almost hit Sophie. The biker's response? Flipping Sophie off. The only rude people in Chicago were the bicyclists. Sophie used to bike before her beloved single-speed was stolen, so she knew that entitlement well. Always wrong, always going too fast to care.

She knew she'd miss that.

The North Avenue bus pulled up to a stop at Milwaukee, right in front of her. Surely, it was a sign she should take the bus. Maybe Fred would be on the bus.

He wasn't, but a homeless man who wouldn't stop staring at her was.

Every woman in Chicago - in any city, really - was used to be ogled by a stranger. It was typically pretty easy to ignore. All you had to do was give a nasty look back and they usually stopped, embarrassed or intimidated.

But this guy didn't. He kept on staring.

He stood by the door in the middle of the bus that was meant for exits. Enter near the driver and pay, exit near the back. Of course, people always exited at whichever exit they felt like and when a stranger who smelled like dried sweat and soil was hovering by that exit the bus patrons certainly didn't feel like exiting out of that particular door.

He wasn't asking anything of anyone. Not money or anything. He was just staring. He did have a small stack of papers in his hand. The papers looked like they were handcut notecards, thin and clipped or torn into the size of rectangular notecards. He lithely passed them to people as they left and some would politely take one and toss it into the garbage the second they stepped onto the sidewalk.

Even though he kept passing out these pieces of paper to everyone who passed by him, his big eyes remained fixed on Sophie. His eyes were wide and black, but not in a scary way. They reminded her slightly of Fred's in that way that felt overly understanding.

The man shuffled over to Sophie's seat. *Not today. Please, no.* Today was supposed to be a hopeful goodbye to Chicago, not a reminder of the slight annoyances that the city could bring.

He stopped in front of Sophie and looked down at her. His whole face looked like it was weighed down. His black hole eyes were the only part of his face that looked upward. He looked at her with the same blank stare he had before.

"No, not right now," Sophie said. "Please."

He held his arm out, handing her a piece of paper. It contained big handwritten block letters in red pen across it, but she didn't want to see.

She shook her head.

He insisted.

"Please, no," she said. *Would no man listen to a woman saying no? Not even a homeless man? Are we all so fucking below them—*

He continued to hold his hand out with the paper facing her. He looked so sad, like he needed her to do just this *one* thing. She felt bad for him. She couldn't remember the last time she really gave a homeless person a chance. She was hardened by so many people on the streets asking for money, asking for time, asking for help. She just kept walking and kept avoiding eye contact.

But this guy's eyes were pleading with her to make contact of any kind.

She took the paper.

"Fire in a woman burns the soul."

Sophie stared at the paper for some time. The small piece of paper was crinkled and worn. She turned it over, but there was nothing on the other side. Only this...what *was* it? Words of warning? Advice? A fortune?

The man took his place back at the bus door, but it was time for Sophie to get off. She felt awful making a scene, telling him to go away and all for nothing. It was just a piece of paper that made no real sense. She fished a dollar bill out of her worn leather wallet and crumpled it up in her palm as she got up. When she stood in front of him she just said, "Here. Take it."

The dollar slipped into his hand like they were making some kind of illicit deal. She rushed off the bus before she could see his reaction.

She got off the North Avenue bus at Sedgewick, where

she stepped directly into a puddle. How was there even a puddle...it didn't matter.

She turned over her shoulder to catch the man's face as the bus rode away. He looked at her bemused, as if she was the one who had done something strange on the bus. She smiled at him and he nodded until his face was out of her vision.

Sophie realized that she hadn't moved out of the puddle. She was still standing there, letting her sneakers drown in muddy sidewalk water. It was all kind of charming, the way that only the ends of things can be. A bittersweet charm that was sending her off onto her next adventure and letting her know that this one was indeed over.

She knew where to go.

She walked up Sedgewick north and turned left on the right street, the one whose name she never memorized, and there was the quiet, idyllic Buddhist Temple. To the right of the temple was the park and on a bench in the park was Fred. He was sitting there, waiting. Fred's deep brown eyes lit up when he saw her. Her grinned with his mouth closed, which felt more touching than a toothy smile

"You figured it out," she said, unable to stop herself from beaming back at him. He figured it out before she did, truthfully, and it was exactly the final sign she wanted from the universe.

"I only spent an entire day anxiously trying to do it, but yes, I did it. I figured it out...even though I was scared I figured it out wrong."

He looked proud of himself for a moment, but his pride slipped back into nervousness as he watched her for a sign of how this interaction might go.

"How long have you been here?" she asked.

"Only an hour."

"And you're still here."

He shrugged. "Where else would I go?"

She put her canvas bag on the ground and sat beside Fred on the bench. The two of them stared ahead for a moment, enjoying this closeness. She wanted to take his hand, but she refrained. She wanted him to talk. Finally:

"Sophie, I have to tell you something."

"I wanted to talk to you, too—"

"I can get you a job at The Onion."

That wasn't at all what she expected him to say.

"Wait - what?"

"Or, I'm pretty sure I can. I can pass your stuff along and set up an interview at least. You're so funny. I'm sure you could do the rest on your own—"

"Oh, Fred. No."

"—No?"

"I mean, I want to do that, yes. But I have to do it myself."

"Well, I would just be helping. You would do the rest yourself. Nailing the job is on you." He laughed nervously and said, "If anything, you could totally botch the interview and give me a bad reputation."

"That's really sweet of you," she said. "But I want to do this on my own and I want to do it my way."

"How very American of you."

"I know, right?"

"But, Sophie, this is how the entertainment business works. You know somebody, you get passed along, you get recommended. No one is just discovered."

She nodded. She knew that. She knew she should take help where she should get it, but she wasn't sure she wanted that job. She didn't think she would be good at it.

"I know you didn't ask me about this, but I thought you might like it."

She reached for his hand and gave it a squeeze. "This was a very nice gesture."

"I hope it wasn't too big or anything."

She shook her head, smiling with a closed mouth like she didn't want to smile but couldn't help herself. It really was sweet.

"But all the same," he continued. "I guess this is more about me. Wanting to keep you around and everything."

"I know. It's just time for me to go."

She rested her head on his shoulder.

"I wish I had met you sooner."

He inhaled deeply, like he was breathing in every last second of the two of them sharing the same air.

"No, this was perfect." She looked at him like she was studying him. She wanted to remember every detail of his face. She wanted to etch his face into her memory like she was carving the details into wood. He interrupted her whittling when he went in for a kiss. Their lips met like memory foam, remembering the curves and textures that they had taken the last month to get acquainted it.

"Besides," he said as he pulled away. "If you had met me like two years ago, you would have hated me. I was soooo in college."

A huge feeling of relief overtook her. Both of them, really. They could feel it. This would be okay. Who knew if it would be forever? Did it have to be forever? Did they have to know there and then what their futures would look like? Did something have to seem like it would work on paper? Couldn't *they* make it work?

"I don't want you to think that I don't support your decision to move."

"I'm still kind of unsure about it—"

"Don't be. You should try it. Even if it's just for a little bit. Otherwise you'll regret it."

"You better be here when I fail."

"What? I'm gonna get a job in LA and move there right

when you move back."

"I'll probably have to move back before the fires get me and the coast drowns."

"In that case, I'll try not to wait that long before I join you."

They laughed softly as if each laugh was a compliment for the other person. He kissed her forehead.

"I'll miss you, Sophie."

She'd miss him, too. So much. Instead of saying that, she said:

"I'm not gone yet."

But he knew what she meant.

NINETEEN

Cafe Mustache was decorated the way it was years ago on her birthday. There was a giant banner across the red curtain on stage that said "good luck". There were balloons on each side of the banner and comics, friends, and acquaintances were hanging Sophie cards that told them how much she would be missed. She was overwhelmed and her goodbye show hadn't even started yet.

Arnie had wanted to throw her a roast - the traditional way to send someone off to a new city - but Sophie felt she had had it hard enough. She didn't need more jokes at her expense, even if they were in good fun and from her best friends.

The audience were in their seats; comics were standing in the back and sitting at the bar. People kept coming up to her to give her a hug. She felt loved - truly loved. Almost in a way that made her not want to leave.

Arnie took the stage - the host of the event - and got ready to introduce Sophie's headlining set. Her last one for a while in her beloved city.

"And now for the woman of the hour. She's my best friend and yours and she is going to crush it in LA. We love you, Sophie. We support you. Now go make us proud and don't you dare come back until you do!"

Sophie smiled, blushing. She could barely look up at the crowd without feeling overwhelmed by all the love. It felt corny, but wonderful. She had never felt such strong acceptance in her entire life.

Of course, this is all happening because I'm leaving.

She glanced at Fred, smiling in the back. They had been inseparable the past three weeks as Sophie prepared her move. He gave her a dorky smile and a thumbs up. What a dork. What a lovable dork.

"Put your hands together for her. It's Sophie Martin!"

She took the stage, beaming from ear to ear. Tears welled her eyes as she looked out into the house at the dark, full crowd. Everyone was there. Every person in the scene. No one was interrupting her to make huge proclamations of love. It was a small, nice gathering with her friends.

"This is really wonderful. Really wonderful. Thank you all."

For a moment she felt sad, knowing she would miss every one of these knuckleheads.

"Hey!" Maura shouted from the bar. "Tell a joke!"

Sophie burst into laughter that shone through the tears that wanted to break down her face.

"Oh, fuck you! We got a heckler, everyone! Luckily, I'm quick on my feet. I've taken an improv class so I know what to do here." Sophie pointed to Maura with her left hand and said, "Zip!"

Everyone laughed politely. Okay, it was time to get into her material.

Only a few days later she was in Los Angeles. It made it feel like her show and her last few months were a dream, but she knew they weren't. She had Arnie texting her every day and Fred calling her almost twice a day to keep her grounded even as she hiked mountains and took in more vitamin D than her Chicago body had ever received.

Sophie was walking up the rocky slopes of Runyon Canyon because she wanted a typical Los Angeles experience with hot people passing her at every dusty turn.

When she stood at a beautiful spot that let her overlook the city, she felt a need to share it with Fred. She wished he was there.

So she called him. She Facetimed him, catching him as he was leaving his office in the gray downtown that was Chicago in March.

"You caught me when I was so perfectly un-showered and gross."

"Fred! You didn't shower for work today?"

"Shhh!"

"Well, I had to show you how actually cool LA looks."

"Wait, where are you?"

"I'm walking."

"No one walks in L.A."

"Well, I do! And I'm going to make you do it, too."

They smiled at each other, looking forward to their next reunion.

"Okay, let me show you my view."

She turned her phone around and let Fred take it all in.

"So it's not so bad there?"

"Well, everyone is way hotter than me, but who am I trying to impress? Except any possible person who can discover me at any given moment."

"Well, I can't wait to see you, my little Angelino."

"I think it's Angelina if I'm a girl."

"You're deliberately missing the point," he said as he got on a train.

"Are you about to talk to me on the El? That's such a faux

pas!"

"I guess you're right, but I love talking to you."

Fred moved his screen around to show Sophie a full train of people at after-work hours going from downtown Chicago to the northside. She was away from Chicago, but she still felt a pang of embarrassment for bothering people on their commute.

"I can wait fifteen minutes for you to get home."

"Okay, you're right. Hey, it's like you said. Some things are worth waiting for."

"I said that?"

"Yeah. About that Prince concert."

"Oh! But that was about Prince."

"Oh, my God, Sophie."

The two of them laughed together, apart.

"Just for that I'm keeping you on the phone," he said, making a face at her that she missed so much.

"Noooo," she protested in jest. But she actually loved it. They were making it work and it was *really* working. For now, at least, and that was good enough. The warm California air felt full of possibility. She felt then with more conviction than ever that even if nothing worked out the way she had dreamt, even if she wasn't a famous comedian, that it would have all worked out in the way it was meant.

OTHER TITLES FROM WEASEL PRESS

Going Somewhere by Joe 3.0

What Makes a Witch by Linnea Capps

Talk Like Jazz by Joseph Cooper

Book of Beasts by Holly Day

The Night at the End of the Tunnel by Mark Greenside

If the Hero of Time was Black by Ashley Harris

In and of Monsters by Kat Lewis

Purple Fantasies by Gary Mielo

Things for Which You Thirst by Claudine Nash

The Escape by Rayah

Miffed and Peeved in the U.K. by Neil S. Reddy

Satan's Sweethearts by Marge Simon & Mary Turzillo

Blood Criminals: Living with HIV in 21st Century America by Jonathan W. Thurston

Once More with Noise by Weasel

CPSIA information can be obtained
at www.ICGtesting.com
Printed in the USA
LVHW110114221222
735707LV00004B/538

9 781948 712613